"Young man—" Evan[...] would have brought Et[...] "Is that a *body*?"

It was obvious that Mick would have given anything in the world to be able to say "No." Numbly, he descended the stairs. "Look," he said, his voice blank with shock, "it's not what you think."

The dead girl was lying across his arms in the Scarlett O'Hara position for the staircase scene, but there were bruises on the bare dangling arms. A thin dark red thread of dried blood streaked from one corner of her mouth. She was very beautiful—and very dead.

Evangeline looked at him sharply. "Just what were you planning to do with her?"

"I thought . . . the back door . . . the garden. Leave her there. After midnight . . . when no one's around . . . move her somewhere else . . . where she could be found. Away from the house . . . away from us . . ."

"Yes," Evangeline agreed, "that might be best. Go out and leave her in the garden, then come back and we'll give you a large brandy. You look as though you could use one."

Bantam Books offers the finest in classic and modern English murder mysteries. Ask your bookseller for the books you have missed.

Agatha Christie

DEATH ON THE NILE
A HOLIDAY FOR MURDER
THE MOUSETRAP AND
  OTHER PLAYS
THE MYSTERIOUS AFFAIR
  AT STYLES
POIROT INVESTIGATES
POSTERN OF FATE
THE SECRET ADVERSARY
THE SEVEN DIALS
  MYSTERY
SLEEPING MURDER

Margery Allingham

BLACK PLUMES
DEATH OF A GHOST
THE FASHION IN
  SHROUDS

Dorothy Simpson

LAST SEEN ALIVE
THE NIGHT SHE DIED
PUPPET FOR A CORPSE
SIX FEET UNDER
CLOSE HER EYES
DEAD ON ARRIVAL

Sheila Radley

THE CHIEF INSPECTOR'S
  DAUGHTER
DEATH IN THE MORNING
FATE WORSE THAN DEATH

John Greenwood

THE MISSING MR.
  MOSLEY
MOSLEY BY MOONLIGHT
MURDER, MR. MOSLEY
MISTS OVER MOSLEY

Ruth Rendell

THE FACE OF TRESPASS
THE LAKE OF DARKNESS
NO MORE DYING THEN
ONE ACROSS, TWO DOWN
SHAKE HANDS FOREVER
A SLEEPING LIFE
A DARK-ADAPTED EYE
  (writing as Barbara Vine)
A FATAL INVERSION
  (writing as Barbara Vine)

Marian Babson

DEATH IN FASHION

Christianna Brand

SUDDENLY AT HIS
  RESIDENCE

R·E·E·L MURDER

A Mystery by
MARIAN BABSON

BANTAM BOOKS

TORONTO · NEW YORK · LONDON · SYDNEY · AUCKLAND

REEL MURDER

*A Bantam Book / published by arrangement with
St. Martin's Press*

PRINTING HISTORY
St. Martin's Press edition published February 1987
Bantam edition / May 1988

Bantam Books are published by Bantam Books, a division of Bantam
Doubleday Dell Publishing Group, Inc. Its trademark, consisting of
the words "Bantam Books" and the portrayal of a rooster, is
Registered in U.S. Patent and Trademark Office and in other
countries. Marca Registrada. Bantam Books, 666 Fifth Avenue, New
York, New York 10103.

PRINTED IN THE UNITED STATES OF AMERICA

KR   0 9 8 7 6 5 4 3 2 1

R·E·E·L
MURDER

CHAPTER 1

There are certain decisions you regret from the moment they are made. By then, it is usually too late.

I knew better. Every time I had fallen into her net, I had lived to regret it. I refused to admit to myself the number of years—decades—it had gone on. It seems that bitter experience teaches us nothing. Or can it be true that some of us are born victims?

"You're an idiot, Mother." My beloved daughter did not hesitate to point this out to me at the airport. (Much too late.) "You know there's trouble every time you have anything to do with her. *She* rushes ahead and does all sorts of awful things—and then you're left holding the baby."

"It's only a trip to London," I defended, glad that she could not read my mind. Poor Martha, she didn't know the half of it. "Two weeks . . . a civilized city . . . everybody speaks English. What trouble could we possibly get into?"

"Practically anything," she said severely. "I'm against this whole trip. I have been since the beginning."

So had I. But I could not possibly admit it now. Besides, Martha was usually against practically anything you could mention.

"Nonsense, dear," I placated. "We'll have a lovely vacation and we'll be back before you know it. You'll see."

"I hope so." There was no hope in her voice, only a grim certainty that I was on a collision course with disaster and about to bring disgrace upon myself and everyone connected with me.

"*Dear* Martha. Still the little ray of sunshine, I see." The bone of contention was upon us. In a *sotto voce* aside to me, she murmured: "*So* like her father. I always warned you *that* was a mistake."

She had her brazen nerve, but there was no time to take

1

issue with her; they were calling our flight. I kissed Martha hurriedly, promised faithfully to write every single day and tell her *everything*, then uncrossed my fingers and followed Evangeline Sinclair into the Departure Lounge.

It was just like old times. First, there were the sideways glances from our fellow passengers, then the furtive nudges, the whispers, and . . .

"*Is* it?" . . . "It can't be." . . . "It *is*—it's *her!*" . . . "She's on our flight! Wait till I tell—" . . .

Evangeline lifted her head higher and passed through the crowd which parted respectfully to allow her passage. She smiled graciously as she met timid eyes, nodded regally to those bolder ones who murmured a greeting. It was an auspicious beginning to our journey.

"My God! Is *she* still alive?" Then some fool spoiled it. "I thought she'd died long ago."

"*Shhhhh!*" But it was too late. There was nothing wrong with Evangeline's hearing. Her lips tightened, her eyes snapped—she'd retained every bit of her legendary temper, too.

"Trixie!" Without turning her head, she summoned me to her side.

"I'm right here." I spoke quietly, both to avert a scene and to counteract the impression she was trying to convey that she was the *grande dame* and I was the walk-on maid.

"Trixie? . . ." I needn't have worried; the whispers started again. "Trixie Dolan?" . . . "Sure, didn't you see her movie on TV last week? *Gold-Diggers of the Great White Way*—that's what they used to call Broadway, back when Broadway *was* Broadway."

Now it was my turn to nod graciously and smile. This was not what Evangeline had intended at all.

"*Dear* Trixie—" I knew I was in trouble. You're always in trouble when Evangeline begins *dear*ing you.

"*Dear* Trixie, it's so kind of you to accompany me on this trip to England. I can't tell you how much it means to me to have one of my *oldest* and dearest friends by my side as Britain honours me."

"It's just a private cinema doing a retrospective season," I said. She could always make me nervous, the way she inflated any attention shown to her. She was making this sound like the female equivalent of a Knighthood, at least. Audiences always did that to her.

"In conjunction with the London Film Festival!" She beamed upon me. "And affiliated with the National Film Theatre. I'm deeply honoured that they should want to do a retrospective of *my* films! I can't think of any Body in the world whose accolade I would treasure more."

And so much for the Metropolitan Museum of Art, which had been annoying her for years by digging up everyone else's films and making a to-do over them.

"Such recognition means *so* much more than the paltry re-runs on the Late Show—"

And so much for me, too.

"Naturally"—she added hastily—"that is not to say that I denigrate television. It has a right and proper place in the scheme of things but—"

The loudspeaker cut across her, requesting that we proceed to the Boarding Gate and board our flight. Not even Evangeline Sinclair could compete with that. Her audience abandoned their fascinated eavesdropping and returned to their own affairs. The pushing and jostling regained its normal level as we struggled forward and eventually found ourselves decanted into the narrow aisles of our prison for the long hours of the flight.

"I can't get over it . . ." Someone was still marvelling. "Evangeline Sinclair and Trixie Dolan—on *our* plane. And travelling together! I mean, wasn't there some big feud? I thought they stopped speaking back in the 'thirties. Or was it the 'forties? There was some hushed-up scandal, anyway. And they had a knock-down drag-out fight and nearly killed each other. . . ." The voice dropped, going into gory details.

There'll always be a film buff. Rumours, half-truths, whispers—they thrive on them. How they love to repeat them with the air of being in the know. I had someone's flight bag knocking the back of my knees and Evangeline immediately in front of me, so I couldn't turn around to see who was speaking. Not that it would have made any difference. This was neither the time nor the place for explanations or corrections.

Especially not the place. We had reached our seats and

Evangeline was frowning. I didn't blame here. I could already feel claustrophobia wrapping its tentacles around me.

"Do they seriously imagine—" her voice rose indignantly—"that anyone larger that a malformed dwarf could endure this seating?"

The appreciative titters of her listeners did not placate her. Her righteous wrath went beyond any satisfaction at providing entertainment. For once, she was oblivious of an audience.

"I'll take the inside seat"—I couldn't stand a scene—not so soon. I pushed past her and curled into the inadequate space. "You can sit on the outside."

"To think—" she mused loudly—"that the French boxcars of World War One were considered so inadequate that soldiers inscribed '40 *hommes, 8 chevaux*' on them. What, one wonders, would those same doughboys say if they could see modern transportation—and realize that people actually *paid* for such accommodation?"

It was no time to remind her that when those same doughboys had left the ground they had often gone up in far worse machines. Not for nothing had they been known as "crates." In fact, looking around, I could see one or two elderly gentlemen who looked as though they might have pioneered air travel—in crates that allowed them little more space than our seating.

"Oh, Ms. Sinclair . . . Ms. Dolan . . ." A flight steward rushed down the aisle towards us. "This is such an honour . . . I'm so pleased to meet you—" He looked at our seats with horror. "But there's been some mistake. Will you come this way, please?"

We struggled out of the seats and followed him to the First Class section. Another film buff doing his bit of homage? Or had he instructions from someone to upgrade us if there was room? It didn't really matter. We settled into seats that were luxurious by comparison with those we had left.

The flight steward bustled behind a curtain and we heard the discreet pop of a champagne cork.

"This is more like it." Evangeline nodded approval.

"Here we are—" The steward was back with two glasses

of bubbling Veuve Clicquot. "We'll finish the bottle after take-off, but that will get you going. You're very lucky. David's piloting this flight. His take-offs are so smooth no one has ever spilled a drop."

"How nice." Evangeline took a deep swallow, making it clear that there wasn't going to be anything left to be spilt on take-off. It seemed like a good idea and I did the same. I don't like take-offs.

"I'll top you up just as soon as we're aloft," our steward promised, leaving us to usher some genuine first class passengers to their seats. Some of them glanced at us with interest, envy and—perhaps—surprise. We were a bit over the usual age for hurtling ourselves around the world.

It seemed no time at all until the engines revved up and we went taxi-ing down the runway, gathering speed. The plane tilted and we were airborne, deep into that first frightening thrust that lifted us into the clouds, leaving—in my case—my heart, stomach and courage still on the ground behind us.

"We're off—" Evangeline drained her glass—"on the Great Adventure."

I wished abruptly that I had never played the lead in *Peter Pan* that season so long ago. As the plane seemed to hesitate and gather itself for the final great thrust into the stratosphere, my mind presented me with that classic finale: the darkened auditorium, the spotlight tight on my face as I lifted my head and "Peter" said,

"To die . . . might be the greatest adventure of all."

CHAPTER 2

I don't mind landings quite so much. Intellectually, I know that they're just as dangerous as take-offs; emotionally, I feel that every foot closer to the ground is a foot closer to safety. I hadn't realized I'd been holding my breath until I expelled it as the wheels touched the tarmac.

"You just stay where you are, ladies, until we get the first rush out of the way," our steward told us. "We have special transport laid on for *you.*"

It was sweet of him to make it sound as though this was going to happen because of our fame and not our decrepitude. Whatever the reason, I was thankful to be spared the long, tedious trudge to the Customs Hall.

"I'm afraid this isn't quite what you're accustomed to," the driver apologized as we sat on the back of his strange little vehicle, gliding past the jet-lagged lines of shuffling travellers.

"Not at all." After a preliminary narrowing of her eyes, Evangeline had decided to be gracious. "I spent a large part of World War II entertaining troops all over the world and jouncing over battlefields in jeeps. This is a far smoother ride."

In fact, I had done a lot more entertaining of troops in far-flung outposts than she had. While she had been mostly behind the lines in the European Theatre of Operations, the USO had assigned me to the Far East—and my jungle jeep rides had been a lot jouncier and more dangerous than anything she had had to face. Both of us had made several tours with Bob Hope; but then, who hadn't?

Someone had collected our luggage from the carousel and it was piled waiting for us in the Customs Hall. It had been a long time since I had had this kind of service. Maybe it was going to be worthwhile travelling with Evangeline, after all.

I changed my mind again when we rolled through the final door, making our entrance to the crowd behind the barrier, a sea of anxious faces straining to watch for the appearance of their own personal star. I heard Evangeline draw in her breath with a hiss of displeasure.

"What's the matter?" My heart sank. It had never taken much to set off that famous temperament of hers.

"Look!" She waved her hand towards the waiting crowd. "Just *look* at that frightful man!"

It took me a moment to spot him; quite a few of them looked frightful to me. Ours was the three-piece-suit, short-back-and-sides generation; multi-hued cockscombs and ragbag raiment held no attraction for me. Then I saw him. No wonder she was furious.

MISS SINCLAIR said the neatly-lettered sign he was holding above his head.

Otherwise, he was a quite unexceptional early-middle-aged man. His suit was conservative, his hair was neatly trimmed, his smile was ingratiating—but he was for ever damned. He had betrayed the fact that he did not expect to recognize Evangeline Sinclair on sight.

Just then, he saw us. His face lit up with relief and he lowered the sign quickly. As he came forward to meet us, he detoured swiftly to drop the sign into a large refuse bin, not knowing it was already too late, poor creature.

"Miss Sinclair, Miss Dolan—" He rushed up to us. "This is a great honour—"

"Yes-s-s-s," Evangeline said.

"How nice of you to think so." I covered quickly, giving Evangeline a dirty look. "And you are—?"

"Oh, forgive me. Hugh. Hugh Carpenter. Let me take your things." He took control of our luggage trolley, swinging it towards one of the exits. "The car is over this way."

I trotted along beside him, trying to keep up a steady stream of small talk in the hope that he wouldn't notice that Evangeline was stalking along behind us in stately silence. Unfortunately, he did.

"Oh, I'm sorry—" He slowed to a snail's pace and gave her another of his ingratiating smiles. "Am I going too fast for you, Miss Sinclair?"

If looks could kill, he would have dropped on the spot.

"Oh, I'm sorry. I didn't mean to imply—" He had already broken off in confusion before I nudged him.

"We're nearly there—" He wheeled the trolley through sliding doors and had second thoughts. "Why don't you ladies wait here and I'll bring the car round? It will be easier now that I know you—I mean, you stay here with the trolley and—I won't be a minute." He abandoned us and the trolley and loped off.

I hoped he was better at driving than he was at diplomacy.

He narrowly escaped being hit by an airport bus and three taxis as he crossed to the car park. I looked up at the towering structure, with its hairpin curves looping up to each level and hoped that he was on the lowest level. It was all too easy to picture him losing control of his car, careering down those steep curves, crashing from side to side until, at ground level, denuded of its fenders and bumpers, the car shot out into the road to collide with a double-decker airport bus.

"Perhaps," Evangeline said thoughtfully, "we ought to take a taxi."

"We can't, really." How I wished we could. "Not after he's gone to all the trouble of meeting us."

"He reminds me of a director I worked with once. We lost three stunt men on that picture."

"Well, he's not directing us, he's only driving us into town—and here he is now."

He drew up to the kerb smoothly and leaped out to come round and open the rear door for us. He handed us into the car, getting it right on the first take, then resumed his seat behind the steering wheel. It was the first indication that there might be hope for him yet.

"Nice car," Evangeline allowed, as we sank back cautiously against the rear seat.

"It's a Rolls-Royce," he pointed out, just in case we hadn't noticed. "Mr. Sylvester has three of them. This is the newest."

"Not . . ." The information seemed to give Evangeline pause. "Not *Beauregard* Sylvester?"

"The one-and-only." Hugh Carpenter turned to beam at us over his shoulder. Three oncoming cars swerved abruptly as we verged perilously near the white line dividing the road and several cars behind us sounded their horns in varying degrees of alarm and indignation.

"I didn't know he was still—" Evangeline broke off and resumed, "How *is* dear Beauregard? I haven't seen him since . . . it must have been . . ."

"*Slaves of Passion,*" Hugh supplied cheerfully. "That was the one the Hays Office tried to ban—" The sudden frost in the atmosphere made itself felt, even to him.

"Yes-s-s . . ." Evangeline said distantly. "*Dear* Beauregard. He taught me so much. But then, he was so much older than I. How *is* he these days?"

"Flourishing," Hugh said. "Surely you must have followed his career, even though your paths divided?"

"Oh, of course . . ." Evangeline said vaguely.

"I'm afraid I lost track of him a bit," I said quickly, knowing Evangeline would never admit to it. We'd never find out anything if I didn't do a bit of tactful grovelling. "Please, just refresh my memory, if you wouldn't mind."

"You probably lost track of him during the war," Hugh said forgivingly. "A lot of people did. He and Juanita Morez—"

"His third wife, I believe." Evangeline remembered that much.

"That's right—and his last." There was a trace of acid in Hugh's voice, perhaps he wasn't as unworldly as he seemed. "They came here in 1937 to make a film for Sir Alexander Korda. An historical romance—"

"He was always at his best with costume dramas," Evangeline murmured. It was not clear whether she meant Sir Alexander or Beauregard Sylvester.

"Was that the one where he played a Cavalier?" A dim memory stirred in my mind. "It kept turning up on the Late Show in the early days of television." In fact, it was one of the group of pictures off-loaded onto the early television companies that had done so much to give English films a bad name.

"That's the one!" Hugh spun the steering wheel expertly

and we slid into the fast lane. "*He Laughed Last*—great, wasn't it? It was such a success that they signed him for another straightaway and rushed it into production. That was *The Merry Highwayman.*"

"Ah yes," I said reminiscently. That had shown up on the late-night shows, too. The reviews had been nearly as pungent as the film.

"He enjoyed working in England—they both did. Juanita was starring in a West End musical comedy. Neither of them really believed there was going to be a war. Even after it was declared, there was that long interval when nothing happened—the Phoney War. Beau signed for another film. Even when Juanita's show was closed when all the theatres were shut down, she didn't care. By that time, she'd discovered she was pregnant and they were so delighted about it, they decided to have the baby here in England and settle permanently. They bought a Regency villa beside the Thames, near to the film studios where Beau was working. Then, of course—"

Evangeline stifled a yawn loudly.

"Forgive me—" He was instantly contrite. "You're both exhausted after your trip and I'm rambling on. Lean back and try to get some rest. We'll be there soon."

"I am not tired," Evangeline said coldly, leaving the implication *merely bored* hanging in the air. She had a low threshold of boredom when the conversation didn't centre on her.

Outside, the fields and factories had given way to little houses, thickly clustered together. As we drove farther in towards the centre of the city, the houses joined together in neat little rows lining the road. Then came concentrations of shops and pubs, each with its own post office and church, set off by yet more little houses. It made me realize the truth of the assertion that London is a collection of villages.

Evangeline was paying no attention to the scenery. Her hooded gaze and withdrawn expression began to make me uneasy. I knew that attitude of old; she was scheming again. And we hadn't even unpacked.

We were passing familiar landmarks now, readily identifiable from stock shots and postcards. Finally, we came to the most famous of all: Buckingham Palace.

"Just a little detour here," Hugh spoke over his shoulder. "I thought you might like to see Buck House."

"Not unless we're staying there," Evangeline said coldly.

"Ha-ha!" He decided to take it as a joke. "I'm afraid we couldn't quite arrange that. Not this time. Perhaps for your next visit."

"Ha-ha," Evangeline echoed bleakly, reminding him that he was lucky she had made it this time. To expect any more trips was tempting fate.

"Yes . . . well . . ." He stepped on the accelerator and we shot down the Mall at a speed I'm sure wasn't allowed. We veered and veered again, skirting Trafalgar Square and heading north.

"Young man—" Evangeline leaned forward suspiciously. "Where are you taking us?"

"To your flat. We'll have you settled in no time."

"You mean . . ." Her eyes narrowed in a danger signal. "We're not staying at the Savoy?"

"Er, no . . ."

"The Dorchester, then."

"Er . . . actually, as you're here for a fortnight, we thought you might be more comfortable in your own flat. A service flat, of course. You'll have everything done for you, just as though you were in a hotel."

"I see . . ." Evangeline looked out of the window and did not appear to like anything she was seeing. "And just where *is* this service flat?"

"Not far now." He swerved round another corner. "St. John's Wood, actually."

"St. John's Wood?" From Evangeline's tone, it might have been Siberia.

"It's not that far out," he said defensively. "It's just above Baker Street."

"I *know* where St. John's Wood is," Evangeline said severely. "It's where Victorian merchants kept their mistresses. In love-nests." She made it sound as though we were being carried away into the White Slave Trade. As though anyone would be interested, at our ages.

"That was a long time ago." Hugh caught the implication; the back of his neck crimsoned. "It's quite respectable now."

"Hmmmph!" Evangeline said.

I wouldn't have thought it possible, but the back of his neck got even redder.

We drove the rest of the way in icy silence.

CHAPTER 3

We turned into a carriageway and pulled up in front of a Victorian edifice, too imposing to be called a mere house, although it must have been once. One of those houses designed to accommodate a family of ten children, assorted elderly relatives and enough servants to ensure that they led the most comfortable of lives.

Today a discreet array of pushbuttons beside an entry-phone grille testified that it had been divided up into apartments—or "Service Flats," as Hugh Carpenter had called them.

I saw the curtains twitch at an upstairs window as we stopped, then Hugh was out of the car and bustling round to open the door for us and help us out.

The front door burst open and a gangling youth stumbled down the steps and lurched to a halt beside us. Evangeline closed her eyes briefly. I managed a smile, but I'd almost forgotten they came so young.

"Help with the luggage, Hugh?" he offered eagerly.

"Good-oh, Jasper." Hugh waved his hand vaguely towards the rear of the car. "It's all in the boot—not locked. Just bring it along, will you?"

Evangeline stood on the paved walk looking up at the house as though all her worst fears had been confirmed.

"Just a few steps—" Unerringly, Hugh Carpenter put his foot in it again. "Not too much for you, is it? Here, take my arm."

Deliberately and ostentatiously, she did not hear him. She drew herself up and mounted the steps swiftly, not even touching the railing. Someday she'd do herself an injury, showing off like that.

I followed her quickly, before Hugh could offer his arm to me. I held on to the railing, but only because I was wearing new shoes with slippery leather soles. Otherwise, I wouldn't have bothered, either.

Evangeline gave an exclamation of annoyance and stopped short. There was a reception committee lurking in the entrance hall. At gaggle of young people in varying stages of what passed for fashion these days were looking welcoming and hopeful as we pushed open the door.

Drama students. I could spot them anywhere.

From behind me, Hugh Carpenter's exclamation of annoyance matched Evangeline's. "That's the flat-share from the top floor," he said. "I've told them not to disturb you. Get along, you lot—" He flapped his hands at them ineffectually, like a man shooing away chickens. "Clear out of here!"

"Weally, Hugh!" A small girl who seemed to have a disintegrating orange haystack, decorated with cerise ribbons, slipping off her head and trailing down her back, spoke haughtily. "I was only passing through on my way to post a letter. There's no need to be wude!"

"I'm not the rude one," Hugh said. "You might at least wait until they were inside the door before you pounced on them."

"Did I pounce?" Haystack quivering perilously, setting cerise ribbons fluttering like exotic butterflies, she turned to us indignantly. "I was mewely on my way out to the postbox. Are we no longer to have access to our own fwont door fwom now on?"

"Be reasonable, Hugh." A young man in a Mohican scalp-lock hairdo with three earrings running up the side of one ear and a multi-zippered black leather outfit, spoke earnestly. "Gwenda's right. We have to live here, too."

"I'm on my way to work—" This one was sleekly-coiffed, her black urchin cut framing her face. Black circles framed her eyes so enthusiastically that she resembled a Panda bear. "Should I have climbed out of the window?"

"I'm not denying your right of access, Ursula," Hugh said reasonably. "I'm simply pointing out that you all might have chosen a better time to converge on the front door. Not very subtle, you know."

Since when had drama students been expected to be

subtle? I'd never met any who were and, for my sins, I taught the occasional course at the local night school. Grabbing attention was the name of the game—and the chance to attract the attention of Evangeline Sinclair must be well-nigh irresistible.

"You're being positively churlish, Hugh." Now a thin wiry boy whose hair stood up in multi-coloured spikes, chimed in. "Leaving these ladies standing in a draughty hallway while you start a *brawl* with the legal tenants. Who do you think you are, the landlord?"

"Des is wight," Gwenda said promptly. "It's disgwaceful of you—and after they've twavelled all this distance. They must be exhausted. The least you could do is let them into their flat before you begin bewating us!"

"Oh, I do apologize." Hugh's tendency to grovel, never far from the surface apparently, rose to the occasion. "What must you think of me? Here. In here—" He fumbled with keys and unlocked a door beside us. "I—I hope it's all right. I mean, you should be comfortable here."

We entered a large drawing-room, dripping with the opulence of a stage setting. Long dark red velvet drapes at the windows, small Persian and Chinese rugs tossed carelessly on top of a wall-to-wall broadloom, huge over-stuffed chairs upholstered in matching velvet, a glorious white marble fireplace and, above it, a gilded Chinese Chippendale looking-glass.

"Aaah," Evangeline said appreciatively. "*The Second Mrs. Tanqueray*, I presume? Or possibly, *Lady Windermere's Fan?*"

"A bit of both," I agreed, just to keep my end up. She knew perfectly well that I'd never acted in a revival of either. You don't get those parts when you have a snub nose and freckles, you have to settle for cute roles. I'd been cute through so many B-pictures I'd made myself sick. She didn't have to rub it in.

"Hmmm . . ." She began strolling around the room, touching the fringe on a lampshade, straightening a silver Art Nouveau picture frame on a rosewood side-table. She looked at the picture in the frame, did a double-take and moved hastily to the mahogany sofa-table behind the sofa.

She reached into a silver rose-bowl and stirred the potpourri inside, releasing a cloud of fragrance into the air.

There was no doubt about it, this room was going to take some living up to. And me without a full-length, bare-shouldered white satin evening gown to my name, let alone in the luggage I'd packed for this trip. Oh well, you can't win 'em all.

"Cwumbs, Hugh!" Gwenda and her friends appeared in the doorway. They had had the forethought to possess themselves of a selection of our luggage and they staggered into the room helpfully. "You've done a gweat job! I wouldn't wecognize the place."

"Now, see here—" Hugh began threateningly.

"How sweet of you, my dears." Evangeline decided to be gracious. Perhaps the room, reeking as it did of *noblesse oblige*, had got to her. More probably, she was doing it to spite Hugh, against whom she had taken one of her unfortunate dislikes. "My bags—thank you so much."

"Where do you want them? The bedwooms?" Gwenda led the way, the others bounding in her wake like over-grown puppies. Evangeline's acceptance of their help had given them new status; if they had tails, they would have been wagging them.

"Where's Jasper?" Hugh called after them. "I thought he was bringing in the luggage."

"Just here, Hugh." Jasper must have kicked the door. It flew open and banged against the wall. He lurched into the room, a suitcase in each hand, a smaller case under each arm. "There's an awful lot of it. I was glad to have some help."

Most of it was Evangeline's, of course. She had made most of her Atlantic crossings in the era when seven days on a luxury liner was par for the course, dressing for dinner every night, plus several changes of costume during the day, plus a spectacular costume for the ship's concert. And that was just the cabin baggage. The serious part of her wardrobe, to be worn once she reached shore, had been packed in cases marked "Not Wanted On Voyage" and stowed away in the hold. There had also been a maid or two to pack and unpack, iron, re-sew buttons, mend torn lace, not to mention waiting on Evangeline hand and foot.

Those days might be gone, but old habits die hard.
Evangeline still packed as though for a year at Court. I'd
thought my poor Martha was going to have a seizure when
she heard how much we were being charged for excess
baggage weight.

"Through there," Hugh directed unnecessarily. Jasper
was already heading for the bedrooms. Our upstairs
neighbours seemed quite familiar with the layout of the flat.
I wondered who had last occupied it.

"Suppose—" Evangeline moved forward. "Suppose *we*
inspect the rest of our quarters?"

"Good idea." I was behind her immediately. If we didn't
make some decisive move ourselves, it was obvious that
Hugh Carpenter was just going to stand around dithering
for the rest of the day.

"Oh, I'm sorry. So sorry." By a series of intricate
sidesteps, he managed to get ahead of us. "The study—" He
snapped a switch and a green-shaded desk lamp glowed
onto the gilt-tooled red leather top of a teak desk.
Booklined walls, armchairs and reading lamps, another,
smaller fireplace, and an enormous window, which didn't
seem to let in much light, on the far wall.

"The conservatory—" Another switch snapped and a
jungle of foliage sprang into view on the far side of the
French windows. White-painted wrought-iron chairs and a
table clustered in a small clearing. "It's a bit hot and muggy
for my taste, but you might like to sit out there occasionally."

"It looks lovely," I said.

"There's another French window in your room that opens
out into it. Your room—" he turned to Evangeline—"opens
into the garden itself, although it's rather chilly at this time
of year. You might prefer to sit in the conservatory, too. It
might remind you of California."

"The California climate does not equate to a steamy,
overheated greenhouse." Evangeline's tone effectively lowered the temperature about ten degrees. "Despite the
untutored opinion of some people. Have you ever been to
California, Mr. Carpenter?"

"Er, no. Not yet, that is. I hope to—"

"You must go sometime. You'll learn a lot."

"Then my room must be through here." I moved ahead hastily, trying to distract Evangeline from her hostilities. It wasn't fair for her to pick on a man she barely knew. I must admit, though, that I had no great faith that Hugh Carpenter would improve on further acquaintance.

My bedroom was plain but pleasant. A faint odour of fresh paint explained Gwenda's surprised reaction on entering the drawing-room. The place had quite obviously been redecorated recently.

"Now—" Hugh looked at the pile of suitcases in the middle of the room. "Are all your bags here?"

"Most of them are Evangeline's," I said. "Those two are mine, but I have two more. Somewhere."

"They must be in Miss Sinclair's room."

"I wouldn't be surprised," Evangeline said. "Everything else seems to be." Everyone else, she meant. We could hear a discrete hubbub from across the hall.

Well! It was definitely the star dressing-room. It had everything but the actual star on the door. By comparison, I was billeted in the broom closet. No wonder the youngsters couldn't tear themselves away from it.

It was twice the size of my room, also freshly painted and wallpapered with a pale gold Regency stripe design. The bed was lengthwise against the lower end wall, framed by pink satin curtains draped Napoleonic-style from a gilt crown just below the ceiling. White-and-gilt-painted bergère chairs with gold velvet cushions, an elaborate chaise-longue, a secrétaire . . . the works! I tried to think what play could have had this for the setting, but was unable to think of any. Unless there'd been a little farce called something like, *Ooh La-La, Joséphine!* which had escaped my attention. There were nearly enough doors for a farce, too.

"This part of the room used to be the morning-room." Hugh moved upstage, to a portion of the room roughly across from the study. "But we knocked down the wall to turn it into one large room. We, er, thought that it might make it more comfortable for—for *you.*"

Hmmmm? That foot was hovering perilously near his mouth again. Just for Evangeline, was it? I began to wonder who might be destined to occupy the star dressing-room after her departure. The flat, in fact. It would make a very nice little love-nest. Was the St. John's Wood tradition lingering on?

"Oh, Hugh—it's fabulous!" Ursula exclaimed.

"Thwilling!" Gwenda glowed with excitement, prowling eagerly around the room. She stopped at the dressing-table, a proper stage dressing-table with the mirror surrounded by light-bulbs. "Where do you—? Oh, I found it!" The bulbs sprang into life and Gwenda bent to pull her hair into yet more separated strands and fluff up her chiffon ribbons. "So this is what all the banging and cwashing was about. Aren't you just wild about it, Miss Sinclair?"

Gwenda? If Hugh had amorous intentions towards her, they certainly didn't show. His face darkened with irritation.

"See here, you lot," he said. "You're becoming tedious. I told you yesterday you weren't to disturb Miss Sinclair—and Miss Dolan. You promised. So much for your promises!"

"Oh, don't be such a wotter, Hugh!" Gwenda pouted.

"*If* we are disturbing anyone—" Ursula spoke with icy grandeur—"we shall leave instantly." She made no move to go.

"We were only helping," Mick, the Indian brave, said defensively.

"We're still helping." Des turned to me. "Point out your cases and I'll carry them to your room for you. Then you can show me which cases belong to Miss Sinclair and I'll bring them back here."

"That's wight!" Gwenda pounced on the idea triumphantly. "We only want to help. We'll do anything at all for you, Miss Sinclair. We'll fetch and cawwy for you, make tea, wun ewwands—" She clasped her hands dramatically. "Just don't send us away!"

"Dear children," Evangeline beamed. "I wouldn't dream of it."

Hugh winced. "On your head be it," he muttered. "You'll have them underfoot day and night."

Precisely what I was afraid of, but Evangeline had the bit in her teeth and there was no stopping her. The double delight of thwarting Hugh and basking in the admiration of young fans was raising her spirits faster than champagne. Besides, it wouldn't be on *her* head, I'd watched her operate before. Evangeline's head was very well trained and could be relied on to produce a shattering headache which required her to go away and lie down quietly whenever a situation became difficult, leaving someone else—anyone else—to cope with the problem. Leaving me.

Again I wondered what momentary madness had led me into agreeing to accompany her. I wasn't in desperate need of a free trip. I could afford to pay my own fare. This way, I was in danger of paying excessively through my nerves. Financially would have been preferable.

"Perhaps they'd like to see the kitchen, Hugh," Jasper said doubtfully. He glanced at us obliquely, as though to make sure we recognized the word.

"Ooh, yes! You must see what they've done with the kitchen." Gwenda led the way eagerly.

"It's quite small," Hugh said apologetically. Just as well. It was the room behind my bedroom and, if it had been much bigger, my bedroom really would have been a broom closet.

"Of course—" Hugh brightened—"you won't be using it much. There are plenty of restaurants nearby and there are also places you can ring up to have a meal delivered. You'll find some numbers by the telephone in the study."

The kitchen seemed even smaller by the time everyone had crowded into it. The youngsters stood looking around avidly, not missing a trick.

"Do you have everything you need?" Gwenda dived for a cupboard beneath a formica work counter. "Pots and pans, yes. Fwying-pan, tea-kettle—" It stood on one of the electric hobs. "Toaster—" It was at the back of the counter. "Supplies—" She opened the fridge. It seemed that quite a domestic heart beat beneath that somewhat bizarre exterior.

"I can assure you," Hugh said frostily, "they have everything they're likely to need."

"Milk, butter, eggs, bacon, ice cubes—" Gwenda called out the inventory, not taking his unsupported word for it. "Well, you have enough for bweakfast, anyway. And if there's anything else you need, you can always bowwow it fwom us. We're wight upstairs—but you don't have to climb them—just give a shout. One of us will hear you."

"You'll have to shout rather loudly, I'm afraid." Hugh gave us a stiff smile. "They're two floors above you—in the maisonette. Jasper has the flat directly overhead."

"That's all right," Jasper said easily. "I can lend them anything they want."

"How kind of you all." Evangeline bestowed approval indiscriminately. "You're making us feel so much at home."

They beamed and wriggled again. Even Jasper was not immune to the Sinclair charm, although he seemed a bit older and more sophisticated than the others. I was relieved to hear that he was directly overhead, it promised a measure of quietness. Of course, appearances were notoriously deceiving and he might play hard rock until three a.m., but somehow I didn't think so.

Des had located a store cupboard and I moved closer to look over his shoulder as he browsed through. We appeared to be well provisioned with tins, jars and boxes of food, including some long-life ready-made dishes. Then the label on one of the tins stood out like a beacon.

It had been a long exhausting flight, my internal clock was completely out of kilter, I was tired and hungry. That was what I wanted now: creamed chicken on toast, a cup of tea—and silence. Especially silence.

This time it was I who did not bother to stifle a yawn.

"There, you see." Hugh rounded on the youngsters instantly. "You're wearing them out. It really is time you left and let them get some rest. You shouldn't be here anyway. You don't see Anni behaving like this."

"Anni's out," Des said, "or she'd be here, too. Anyway," he added meaningly, "she's already had a chance to see all the alterations."

"P'waps we *should* go now—" Gwenda glanced uneasily at Evangeline, who was smiling bravely but seemed to be growing frailer before our eyes. I was still working on that one, but she had it down pat. On her better days, she could even go pale at will.

"Dear children," Evangeline said weakly. "You have been so kind. You must come down and have a glass of sherry with us some time. If we have any sherry . . ."

"If you haven't, we'll bwing some!" All the cerise ribbons fluttered wildly as Hugh herded them toward the exit. "And don't forget—if you want anything, just shout."

"I may even scream," Evangeline said between clenched teeth as the door closed behind them.

"I'm terribly sorry about that." Hugh was still inside with us. "I *told* them they mustn't disturb you."

"'Stand not upon the order of your going—'" Evangeline fixed him with Lady Macbeth's demented gaze. "'*But*—'"

He went. "We'll be in touch tomorrow. . . ." floated back over his shoulder.

I opened the creamed chicken and we had our light meal, did some unpacking, and roamed aimlessly through the flat in the restless jet-lagged state when you feel it's too early to give in and go to bed, but can't settle to doing anything useful.

"There must be a television set somewhere," Evangeline grumbled, opening doors and drawers in her bedroom. "There's everything else."

"Let's try the drawing-room." We roamed back there and stood looking around. "Now, where would I hide a television if I were a set designer?" I crossed to a promising-looking cabinet and opened it. "Nope, that's the bar."

"That will do." Evangeline revived a bit and began pulling out glasses and a decanter of brandy. I crossed to the matching cabinet.

"Ah—here it is!" It only took a few more minutes of experimentation before I found the proper switch and the set came to life. Meanwhile, Evangeline had poured our drinks, settled herself in an armchair and begun a dissection of our new friends upstairs.

"She's a sweet child, but seriously deluded, I fear. How can she hope to get anywhere in the theatrical field with a speech impediment like that?"

". . . in the city. But we can expect—" On the television screen, a man in front of a weather map leaned forward and confided—"thwee degwees of fwost in the outlying suburbs."

We stared at each other, dumbfounded. Evangeline shuddered and took a deep gulp from her glass.

"Forget I mentioned it," she said.

I did, but I remembered something else I had intended to check out. Casually, I drifted over to the rosewood side-table and picked up the silver Art Nouveau picture frame. As I had suspected, the face was familiar.

"Isn't this Beauregard Sylvester?"

"I wondered how long it would be before you spotted that." Evangeline took another deep gulp of brandy. "We must face it: we have been delivered into the hands of the Enemy!"

CHAPTER 4

The cerise chiffon bows on my tap shoes kept coming undone and flapping all over the place. Busby Berkeley was furious with me. The rest of the chorus line was giggling and the star accused me of trying to upstage her.

"It won't do you any good," she snarled. "You'll just wind up on the cutting-room floor—where you belong!"

I was being my cutest, but it wasn't doing me any good. It was all a nightmare.

It was with relief that I heard the strange insistent noise summoning me back to consciousness and reality. I lay with open eyes staring into blackness while my mind caught up with me and told me that I was in England and the odd *brrr-brrr* noise that wouldn't stop was the telephone on my bedside table. I groped for it, knocking something unidentifiable off the table—I hoped it wasn't the lamp.

"Yes, yes. I mean, hello. Who is it—?" I groped again, this time connecting with the lamp and switched it on. "Who—?" I blinked, covering my eyes against the sudden brightness.

"Who is it?" another voice demanded. It wasn't mine. "Do you realize what time it is?" I recognized Evangeline's indignant tones.

"Get off the line!" Another indignant voice snarled back at her. "I'm calling my mother. What are you doing answering?"

"Martha—" I groaned, finally identifying the distant voice. "Why are you calling at this hour?" I blinked at my watch and it swam into reluctant focus. "It's four o'clock in the morning. What's the matter? What's wrong?"

"Matter?" she wailed. "Wrong? That's what I want to know. You never called me. Did the plane land safely? Are you all right?"

"Don't be absurd!" Evangeline snapped from her exten-

24

sion. "If anything had happened to that plane, you'd have heard about it. It would have made headlines all over the world."

"But anything could have happened after you landed. There could have been an automobile accident—"

"Nonsense," I said quickly, before Evangeline could. "Hugh is a very careful driver. We were perfectly safe."

"Hugh? Who's Hugh?"

"Hugh," Evangeline said icily, through clenched teeth, "is an English gigolo who swept your mother off her feet the moment she arrived. I had to forcibly remove him from her bedroom just a few hours ago. All your worst fears are realized. If you value your inheritance, you will rush over and join me in the unequal struggle to keep your lust-ridden mother from the arms of this fortune-hunting monster."

"Mother!" Martha wailed. "Mother—!"

"For heaven's sake, Martha, pull yourself together. How can you be so gullible! You can't possibly imagine—"

"Oh, can't she?" Evangeline chuckled wickedly.

"Mother—" Martha wailed again. "Mother, don't do anything rash. Promise me—"

"Martha, don't be so stupid! You can't believe—"

"He's very handsome, I'll admit," Evangeline said insidiously. "And you know how susceptible your mother always was."

"Mother—!"

"Evangeline—get off the line! This is my call!"

"I'll do my best, Martha, but you know your mother. There are times when there's just no holding her."

"Mother—!"

"Evangeline—hang up!"

"You mustn't blame her, Martha. It's just the way she's made. *Made* being the operative word, of course."

"Mother—!"

"Evangeline, I'm going to kill you!" At last, I was awake enough to realize the futility of shouting into a telephone when two raving egomaniacs were on the line. I set down the receiver on the bedside table, shuffled into my slippers and went across the hall into Evangeline's room.

"Oh yes, Martha. At your age, you may not believe it,

but one is never too old to hope for romance. You have to face it, Martha—" Evangeline was still having her fun. "A glamorous foreign city . . . away from all restraints . . . a young handsome man making eyes at her . . . She wasn't the first, and she won't be the last—"

"Mother—!"

"All right, that's enough!" I slammed my fingers down on the telephone cradle, cutting her off. "You ought to know better! How dare you upset Martha like that? You know she's a bit naïve?"

"Naïve?" Evangeline snorted. "Face it, Trixie—you're seventy-five years old and your only daughter is a gibbering middle-aged idiot!"

"I'm only sixty-eight," I said coldly. "And Martha is forty. That's hardly middle-aged these days. Besides, she means well. She has my best interests at heart."

"Hmmph!" Evangeline settled back against the pillows. "You should have beaten her more when she was a child."

"If I had, she'd probably be writing a book about it now."

"She may be doing that anyway."

"You should talk! You're old enough to have outgrown the mischief-making stage. You must be eighty now—or is it eighty-five?"

"I haven't decided recently," Evangeline said thoughtfully. "Which do you think is more effective? Or maybe I should stick at seventy-six for a few more years?"

I snorted in my turn and stormed back to my own bedroom. The telephone was still projecting strange ululating noises. I picked it up carefully and held it to my ear.

"Mother—" Martha wailed. "Mother—speak to me!"

"Oh, shut up!" I snarled and slammed down the receiver.

My second awakening was more peaceful. There was no sound from Evangeline's room and the clock told me it was ten a.m. With luck, I might have some time to myself before she awoke. I rose and went into the kitchen to put the kettle on.

A woolly white cloud seemed pressed against every window. When I got closer to a window, the cloud receded a bit and I was able to look out into a hazy landscape which must have been charming when the sun was shining. As it was, blurred by fog and with droplets of moisture clinging to every leaf and twig, it had an enchantment of its own. November fog and an autumn garden, grey-green and brown, softly evocative of loss, mystery, adventure—perhaps danger. What a waste to have a setting like that and no camera to capture it, no actors to begin the promised drama.

Abruptly, I remembered just what it was like to be acting out-of-doors on location in a setting like that: the damp chill creeping into your bones while you waited for the dozens of technicians to arrange and rearrange their bits; the endless retakes while you grew colder and wetter, until your fingers were too numb to hold the props and your brain too numb to remember the dialogue. No, the garden could remain an empty setting, a lost location, for all I cared now. Those days were long behind me. I hadn't thought of them in years.

The kettle began whistling shrilly and I rushed to turn it off before it woke Evangeline.

"Hmmph!" Too late. She made one of her Entrances—so she was in that mood today—drawing her heavy black velvet robe closer around her and doing up the gold braid frogs and clinching her waist (still a trim one) with the heavy gold cord.

"Good morning, Evangeline." She made me feel like a frump in my quilted glazed cotton housecoat—so carefully chosen for me by Martha last Mother's Day. It had been easier to pack it, bulky though it was, than try to explain to Martha just why I didn't want to bring it along. I resolved to get to Harrod's at the first opportunity (preferably without Evangeline) and buy myself something decent.

Evangeline seated herself at the tiny table and looked around fretfully. When I didn't move, she got up again, found herself a cup and saucer, the jar of instant coffee and made her own coffee.

"Toast?" I asked as the toaster popped; there were two slices in there anyway.

"Oh, all right," she said, doing me a favour.

I put two more slices of bread into the toaster. They were the thinnest slices I had ever seen, so thin that the two that had just popped up were crisped all the way through.

Evangeline munched absently, looking out at the fog-shrouded garden, thinking her own thoughts.

"The garden must have been lovely in the summer," I said. "It's sort of pretty and atmospheric now—in a spooky kind of way."

"Spooky is right." Evangeline frowned out at the fog. "It looks like a good place to bury a body."

"Trust you to think of that!" Evangeline's long and chequered career had starred or featured her in every possible kind of film—some of which she hoped everyone had forgotten. These days she had cornered the market in Ethel Barrymore-type roles. There wasn't a regal dowager fighting for what she believed to be right, a proud matriarch struggling to hold her family together against the odds, a society doyenne adrift in a new social order, an unforgiving dying millionairess surrounded by her unloving relatives, that Evangeline hadn't played in the past couple of decades. (We will draw a merciful veil over that sixties horror film where she prowled the dark old mansion as the psychotic aunt, despatching family and servants with an electric carving knife, and hurtled down the staircase to her well-deserved sticky end after tripping over the extension cord.)

"What's that?" There had been a sharp metallic click from somewhere at the front of the flat. My nerves weren't as on edge as Evangeline's appeared to be, but we both went to investigate.

At the end of the tiny vestibule, two square white envelopes lay just inside the door beneath an oblong slot in the door that I had not noticed last night.

"It's just the mail," I said thankfully. I didn't feel strong enough to cope with anything more vital. From the hallway outside, we heard the front door close firmly.

I stooped and gathered up the envelopes while Evangeline went on into the drawing-room. There was one for each of us, but I noticed there was no stamp or franking on the envelopes. They had been delivered by hand, then; presumably by the person who had just left.

Evangeline was standing at one of the drawing-room windows, looking out at the circular carriageway. I joined her just in time to see a tall dark shape walk into the mist at the end of the carriageway and disappear on the other side of the wall that bordered the property.

"The one called Jasper, I believe," Evangeline said. "He looks different in the daylight."

"If you can call this daylight." The fog seemed even thicker at the front of the house. Disconcertingly, it seemed to be alive. It thickened and thinned capriciously, one moment giving us a clear view of the cluster of rose-bushes in the centre of the drive, the next moment obscuring the entire world. I began to appreciate the fine discipline of dry ice clouds wafting across a sound stage.

Heavy footsteps thundered down the hall stairs from the top floor, paused at the landing above, then descended more slowly and quietly. Someone had obviously taken sudden thought of the two elderly ladies in the ground-floor flat.

Again the front door closed quietly and a figure stood on the top step squinting into the fog.

"Who's that?" Evangeline frowned. "How many people do they have living in that top flat, anyway? It must be crowded."

"I think . . . Yes, it is. It's Des, but he's done something to his hair."

"He must have. He looks quite normal."

"Crestfallen, in fact." He had washed the multicolours out of his hair and his spikes had been flattened down to a rather uneven, but unremarkable, style. "So that's what they do with it when they want to go out to work." He was carrying a clarinet case and would not now look out of place in an orchestra.

"He's the sensible one. There's not much that other boy can do about his Mohican cut—except wait for all the shaved parts to grow back."

"Ah, the Indian scalplock!" Evangeline sighed reminiscently. "I haven't seen a style like that since *The Revenge of the White Squaw*. How it takes me back. Now, *that* was a picture!"

"They don't make them like that any more," I agreed. They wouldn't dare. The title alone would make it impossibly racist and sexist today. I wondered whether they would be showing it in the Retrospective or whether all that violence would rule it out. I'd heard the English were more sensitive than we were to things like that.

"It was a classic," Evangeline said complacently. "Do you know, even today I have people coming up to me and telling me that they can still hear the scream I gave when the Indian squaws threw the broken body of my little son at my feet. They don't realize that it was a silent film. They *heard* my emotion. *That* was acting!"

"You had faces then," I said, but it went straight over her head.

"*And* we knew how to use them. We didn't rely on outrageous costumes and silly hairstyles. *Look* at him. You could pass him in the street and never notice him without his—his plumage."

"Perhaps that's why he does it. This generation knows how to use its plumage."

Walking down the carriageway, Des twitched uneasily and looked back over his shoulder, as though subliminally aware that he was being watched and discussed.

On impulse, I pulled back the curtain and gave him a smile and a cheery wave. His face brightened instantly, he returned the smile and wave and disappeared into the fog, a jaunty spring now in his step.

"Well," Evangeline said drily, "that's your good deed for the day."

I got that impression myself. I was further bemused by the discovery that Des had a lovely smile—and that this was the first time we had seen it. Come to think of it, none of the youngsters—for all their high spirits and eagerness to meet us—had seemed especially happy yesterday.

"Well," Evangeline said brusquely. "Are you going to stand around mooning all day, or are you going to give me my letter? Our marching orders, I'll be bound. We might as well know the worst."

"Oh, it's not so bad—" I tore open the envelope and scanned the brief lines. "Lunch with Beauregard Sylvester at the Ivy at one. I presume yours is the same. A car will call to collect us."

"Lunch . . . with Beauregard Sylvester . . ." Evangeline made it sound like a date with the tumbrils. "I do

believe I'm getting one of my splitting headaches. You'll
have to go without me."

"Oh no you don't!" She wasn't going to start getting away
with that again. "He was *your* co-star in all those pictures.
You're going to have to meet him sometime. You can have a
couple of aspirins and lie down for a while—but we're both
going to that lunch!"

CHAPTER 5

There were palm trees growing in the forecourt of St. John's Wood underground station. Even Evangeline took that as a good omen as we drove past, although she had to be snippy about it.

"A bit stunted, aren't they?"

"We used to have much bigger ones," Hugh said, "but we had an exceptionally severe winter a few years ago and they died. These are the replacements. They'll grow."

"I think it's marvellous that you have any at all," I said. "I never thought the climate was tropical enough for palms."

"It's not tropical, but it seldom gets so Arctic that they can't survive. The Gulf Stream, you know. It flows offshore and protects us from the worst of the cold and storms. Usually."

"Good heavens," Evangeline gasped. "What's that?"

A gleaming gold dome was drifting in the fog, a tall stone minaret beside it. For a moment, it seemed that we might have taken the wrong turning and were approaching Baghdad.

"That's the Regent's Park Mosque." Hugh identified it calmly. "We have a large Islamic community now, you know."

"London has certainly changed since the days when I knew it." Evangeline was pensive. "Perhaps I shouldn't have stayed away for so long. Everything seems so strange now."

"Wait until we drive through the City," Hugh said. "Then you'll really see some changes."

"At least," Evangeline said with satisfaction, "some things don't change."

The Ivy was an opulent rendezvous in a side street off Cambridge Circus. Across the street from it, a theatre

32

proudly proclaimed that *The Mousetrap* had been running for four decades.

Inside, there were shaded lamps, oil paintings on the walls, small bronze sculptures in every niche and in front of the dark mullioned windows. It was quiet and luxurious, the food was delicious. You could look around and imagine that Binkie and Gertie and Noel were about to make an entrance at any moment.

Beauregard Sylvester was a poor substitute. I was beginning to feel a headache of my own coming on. I sat there wondering why I had misspent any of my early teenage years being madly in love with his inflated image on the screen at Saturday matinees.

His profile was just as devastating as it had been, despite the fine network of wrinkles. The shock of thick wavy hair had turned an impressive solid silver. The dark penetrating eyes still seemed to suggest that, if only he weren't an honest man and totally devoted to his wife, you might be the lucky lady he swept across his saddle horn and rode off into the sunset with. The deep haunting power of his voice had not waned with the years; you could listen to it for ever—if only you didn't have to pay any attention to what it was saying.

That was the trouble. I stiffened my jaw against another yawn. Beauregard Sylvester might have been a star, but he only twinkled when someone else had written the script. There were a lot of them about.

"Juanita's certainly going to be sorry she missed this lunch, but she's in the country, you know."

We did know. At a conservative estimate, it was the fifth time he'd told us. If Juanita were going to be all that upset, it would have seemed that she might have made an effort to come up to town and join us.

"She doesn't get up to town much," he said again. "She's become a real little country mouse."

If that were true, she had sure changed her spots since the old days. On the other hand, it occurred to me that, if I had been married to Beauregard Sylvester for fifty years (which heaven forbid!) I might want to put some country miles between us, too.

"Dear Juanita," Evangeline said absently. "It will be so nice to see her again—after all these years."

"She hasn't changed a bit" he testified promptly. "Of course," he added belatedly, "neither have you."

"Dear Beauregard, always the Southern gentleman."

"It's true, my little *Flower of the North*." He gave her the same look he had given her in the film of that name when, as a nurse with the Yankee army, she had steadfastly tended his wounds, hiding the fact that he was a Confederate officer to save him from being shot as a spy, and they had fallen in love, defying the prejudices of both sides and, as the cruel Civil War ended, they married and joined a wagon train to start life afresh in the newly opened Western Territories.

"Mmmm." The look left her considerably less moved in real life than it had on celluloid. I now suspected that had always been the case.

Even Hugh Carpenter seemed depressed. I caught him sneaking a look at his watch. It was probably a dirty trick, but I made a point of catching him. Anything to get us out faster.

"Are we keeping you from something, Hugh?" Beauregard Sylvester followed my gaze and noticed that part of his audience was restless.

"Oh, er, no—" Hugh jumped. "No, er, that is, I was just wondering if the programme had started yet. I'm sure the ladies are anxious to see The Silver Screen in the Sky at Cinema City. It's quite impressive, you know." He turned to us. "And the afternoon programme starts in half an hour. We'd just have time to make it comfortably if we were to leave now."

"But we haven't had our dessert yet." Beauregard was close to outrage. "It's part of the set lunch. We're paying for it."

Evangeline closed her eyes briefly and I remembered that rumour had always had it that Beauregard Sylvester was the slowest draw in the West when it came to drawing a billfold instead of a gun.

"Oh, sorry. Yes, of course." A waiter materialized beside the table and Hugh turned on him as though it was all his fault. "May we have the sweet trolley?" he asked brusquely.

The waiter moved off and returned pushing a hostess cart loaded with luscious desserts. There was no question here of picking something at random from a printed menu, it was spread out temptingly before you.

There were profiteroles heaped beside a bowl of dark rich chocolate sauce, cakes crowned with towering peaks of whipped cream, and the golden mounds topped by glittering caramelized sugar of *crème brulée*. The most innocent item was a bowl of fresh fruit salad, but it was dredged deep in Kirsch and a pitcher of heavy cream lurked beside it. I could feel my waistline expanding even as I looked at it all.

"Beau, darling—fancy meeting *you* here!" Cecile Savoy —Dame Cécile of recent years—*grande dame* of the British stage, caught our host's neck from behind in a sort of modified half-Nelson and bussed him on the cheek.

"Hello, Cec," he said without any great enthusiasm. "You remember Eve Sinclair, don't you?"

"How could I forget her and that wonderful season when we lit up the West End in *Three On A Match*? How are you, Evangeline?"

"Very well, Cecile, and you?"

Their implied rebukes to Beauregard Sylvester at the way he had shortened their names went right over his head. He was frowning at the sweet trolley as though the decision he had to make was of vital importance to the world.

"And *how* is darling Juanita?" Dame Cecile asked, a wealth of private meaning quivering beneath her dulcet tones. "Still cloistered away in the country?"

"You know she hates to come up to town these days." Beau was obviously having a struggle to answer politely. "What are you doing here, anyway? I thought you were working."

"Still in rehearsal, we don't open for another week. I *do* hope you'll all come to opening night?"

"We're already booked," Hugh assured her. "All of us." He glanced at us. "I haven't had time to mention it."

"Why aren't you rehearsing now?" Beau wanted to know.

"Aah!" Dame Cecile trilled, waving a hand. "Fortunately—for us, if not for him—the Director was struck down by a toothache. He's rushed off to the dentist, so the rest of us have a free afternoon. Isn't that lucky? Otherwise, we wouldn't have run into each other here."

"Very lucky indeed," Evangeline said, "although I *was* planning to telephone you as soon as we got settled. We only arrived yesterday."

"*And* we'll get together—soon. Well—" Dame Cecile paused and caught Evangeline's eye in what was obviously an old signal. "Well, I must just go and fix my hair before I meet my nephew."

"That's not a bad idea." Evangeline rose to her feet swiftly. "I'd like to freshen up myself. You can show me where it is."

I struggled to get up, but Evangeline's hand was on my shoulder, firmly pushing me back into my chair. I got the message. I was supposed to stay here while they went and had themselves a grand old gossip in the powder room.

"But," Beau protested, "what about your dessert?"

"I don't want any," Evangeline said carelessly. "I'll just have a coffee when I get back."

"Coffee is extra," Dame Cecile murmured under her breath. They swept across the room and up the staircase in gales of laughter.

"Those two always were as thick as thieves." Beauregard Sylvester stared after them broodingly. "Aren't you going with them?"

"I'm fresh enough," I said. It was a line from *Gold Diggers Strike It Rich*. I had brought the house down with it then, now only Hugh raised a wintry smile of recognition.

"She's a Dame now, you know." Beau was still brooding. "The Queen gave her that award."

"She's English." Hugh spoke with the patient weariness of one who had explained it many times. "Those awards are given to British subjects."

"Douglas Fairbanks, Jr. got a knighthood—and he wasn't a British subject. He wasn't living in this country as long as I've been, either. How do you explain that?"

"I don't know how to explain it." Hugh's spine abruptly stiffened. "I don't *have* to explain it. It's nothing to do with me. Honours are bestowed at the discretion of the Government—"

I let my spoon do a little tap dance over the hard shiny

shell of my *crème brulée*—it was probably the least caloric item on the trolley, especially if I cracked the shell and picked it off.

Complaint and counter-complaint droned on over my head; it was very boring. I would much rather be upstairs in the powder room listening to all the lovely gossip and intrigue. Anyway, I'd learned one thing from Dame Cecile's parting sally: Beauregard Sylvester had carried his West Coast reputation over here with him. He was obviously as slow with a pound as he had been with a dollar.

And Evangeline would never tell me all the juiciest bits of gossip, she never did. She'd only tell me the unimportant bits. Anything really interesting I'd have to find out for myself.

I was still in a modified sulk when Evangeline came back to the table looking as though she had eaten several canaries. If she'd hiccoughed, feathers would have floated from her mouth.

"Dear Beauregard," she trilled. "Are we ready to go now? I'm simply dying to see your dear little cinema. I've been hearing such fascinating things about it."

Beau shot her a suspicious look. "Like what?"

"Oh . . . things . . ." Evangeline had slipped into one of her most maddening moods.

"Like what?" Beau's nostrils flared dangerously and his eyes narrowed in the look that had struck terror to the hearts of evil-doers in every film he had ever made.

"*Interesting* things." Evangeline was not an easy woman to terrorize, perhaps because she had done her own share of it in her time.

"Right." Hugh lurched to his feet, nerves cracking under the strain. He showered cash upon the table while Beau was still trying to extract a credit card from his wallet. "Let's be on our way."

Naturally, this restored Beau's good humour. He replaced his wallet far more quickly than he had drawn it out and even held the door for us as we went out. If he had a momentary impulse to let it slam in Evangeline's face, he restrained himself. But the day was young yet.

Unwittingly, he got his revenge when we reached the cinema. I thought Evangeline was going to have a seizure

on the spot. Obviously, this was one item of news Dame
Cecile hadn't imparted to her.

We had pulled up at the entrance to Cinema City, an
impressive skyscraper on the border of the City of London
and Evangeline had stood on the pavement for a moment
looking up at the building with a smirk of private knowl-
edge. Then Beau had rushed us through the lobby, into one
of the elevators and whisked us directly to the penthouse
cinema on the roof.

The elevator decanted us into a large padded cell. On
closer inspection, it turned into a lush foyer with thick
carpeting—on both floor and walls. A ticket booth faced the
elevator and—I blinked—several Mack Sennett Bathing
Beauties in full costume lounged beside the refreshment
concession.

It had stopped Evangeline dead in her tracks, too. While
we absorbed this phenomenon, something suddenly struck
me as very familiar about the straw-coloured locks escaping
from the mob-cap style bathing hat of one of the Bathing
Beauties.

"Oh, Miss Sinclair, Miss Dolan—" She rushed forward to
greet us. "Welcome! Welcome to the Silver Scween. We're
so thwilled—so honoured! Come and see the stills—" She
took Evangeline's hand and tugged her over to a display.
"See—you're the next attwaction."

That was when I thought Evangeline was going to have a
seizure. There it was, staring out at her from behind the
glass:

> She put the SIN in Cinema! Eve Sinclair—as
> you've never seen her before . . . sins across the
> sky in . . . WHEN ANGELS FALL

Beneath the legend, in full blazing colour, sprawled Eve
Sinclair (in the days before she had gone formal both as to
name and as to decorum) in ripped bodice, displaying
heaving bosom, cringing in wild-eyed terror with a flaring-
nostrilled male (not, in this case, Beauregard Sylvester)
looming over her.

Yep, there it was: the poster for the film her fourth

husband had spent a large chunk of his fortune trying to suppress.

"You——" Evangeline gasped, her hand fluttering to her throat. "You actually have a *print* of that? A *complete* print?"

"Almost complete—and restored in our own laboratory," Beau affirmed proudly. "We caught it just in time. All those early films on nitrate stock are disintegrating, you know."

"So I'd heard," she said faintly. She had hoped for nothing more. "But *wherever* did you find it?" (She had thought that every available copy had been bought up by that fourth husband and burned or buried in the depths of an abandoned mine somewhere in Nevada.)

"It was sheer luck. Hugh discovered it on a trip to Hong Kong. There were rumours that it had come from Mainland China. He bought it from the guy who had it and brought it back here where we started on the restoration work right away. Good Old Hugh."

"Anyone would have done the same," Hugh said modestly, blissfully unaware that he had nothing to be modest about.

"Isn't that a fantastic rescue story?" Beau, too, was inordinately pleased with himself. "You'd hardly believe it—except that the print still has Chinese subtitles running down the side. Ursula—she's our archivist—did her best, but we couldn't get rid of them without ruining the print."

"That's right," Hugh chimed in eagerly. "Ursula's the best we have at restoration work but even she couldn't do it. The only way would have been to black them out and then we'd have lost the action running underneath."

"What a pity," Evangeline said. Nothing would have suited her better than to have the entire film blacked out. She wanted everyone to forget the days when she had been billed as the sexpot who "put the Sin in cinema." (Not a few people opined that she had also done a lot towards putting Hays in the Hays Office.)

Still, I had some sympathy for Evangeline in this situation. There were certain of my own films I'd be happy to think had self-destructed, particularly a top contender for the Golden Turkey Award called *No More Sugar For Daddy*, complete with title song. I must admit that when I occasionally fell over the old 78 disc at a bazaar or flea market, I bought it up, took it home and had a smashing good time with my little hammer.

"Come and see the view from the roof garden." Beau led the way to a door on the far side of the lobby. We stepped through it into an English garden—twenty-five storeys above the ground. The tables and chairs, when looked at closely, turned out to be heavy white plastic replicas of the usual wrought-iron garden furniture. At the moment, they were heavily beaded with damp and there were no customers for the small bar built out from the side of the cinema.

"We're getting one of those retractable plastic roofs, like they have on the QE2, to roll out when it rains, so that we can enjoy the garden in all weather."

"What a good idea," I murmured as Evangeline continued to brood over what she undoubtedly saw as a betrayal.

"Look over here." Beau led us down a squidgy gravelled path between dispirited brown stalks with shrivelled leaves hanging here and there, to a rustic bower at one corner of the roof. "Isn't that a view to end all views?"

We looked down on a bank of fog that seemed solid enough to step out on.

"It certainly is," Evangeline said tartly. "I haven't seen anything like it since the fog-making machine went out of control when we were shooting *Beast of the Barbary Coast*."

"Oh, well," Beau said, "I'm afraid it's not a very good day today. But when it's clear, you can see the Thames, the Tower of London, Tower Bridge. . . ." He went on pointing out invisible sights while we shivered in the dank chill.

"Perhaps—" Hugh finally noticed a particularly convulsive shudder of Evangeline's—"perhaps we ought to go in now. It's cold up here."

"And getting windy," I said. The sooner they got that plastic roof, the better, although I wouldn't like to take any bets on how long it would last if the wind was often this strong. It wasn't going to do the flowers any good, either.

"I think the wind's blowing the fog away a bit." Beau held his ground stubbornly. "If you lean over the parapet just a little—" he illustrated; none of us rushed to join him—"and look over that way, you ought to be able to see the top of Tower Bridge."

Evangeline looked wistfully at Beauregard Sylvester's broad back as he leaned out. Her hands twitched briefly and I saw the struggle as she got her impulses under control. Besides, there were too many witnesses.

"No, I'm afraid the fog isn't really clearing all that much." Unaware of his narrow escape, Beau straightened up and stepped back from the parapet into the precarious shelter of the rustic bower. "Next time you come, the weather ought to be better."

Neither of us answered. We were too busy racing each other across the roof, back to the warmth of the cinema lobby. I was through the door ahead of Evangeline, which was just as well because I'd never have had the nerve to let the door slam in Beau's face the way she did.

"You poor angels, you must be fwozen! Come and have some coffee. Would you like a little bwandy in it?"

I had liked that girl from the moment I saw her. Her hair might resemble an abandoned bird's-nest, but her heart was in the right place—and there was nothing wrong with her brain, either.

"We'd love some," I gasped, checking to see whether my fingers had actually turned blue or just felt as though they had.

"With a *lot* of brandy in it," Evangeline amended, flexing her own fingers. "On second thought, you can forget the coffee."

"Sorry—" Hugh grimaced apologetically—"but we're ruled by licensing hours. Not only that, but the matinee is about to let out. If people think the bar is open—" He grimaced again.

"I see." Evangeline plainly saw that the world was aligned against her. Her martyred heroine expression returned.

"There isn't *much* coffee." Gwenda was back with a tray of coffee cups and saucers. She spoke the literal truth. There was only enough coffee to colour the brandy.

"Thank you, dear." Evangeline sipped appreciatively. "How this takes me back—" She looked into her cup reflectively. "Just like a Speakeasy during Prohibition days."

Two usherettes secured the doors back and the first stream of departing cinema-goers poured across the lobby towards the lifts, chattering, struggling into their coats and blinking in the light. Several of them glanced at our little group and nudged each other. I wondered if it were entirely fortuitous that we were there at that time. Had Beau deliberately lingered over dessert so that we could become an added attraction for the matinee audience?"

"Drink up," Beau said heartily. "The next show starts in fifteen minutes."

I noticed now that the lifts were disgorging as many as they had engorged. A queue was forming at the ticket office. Gwenda had hurried away to help behind the candy counter, where they were also selling hot coffee and some amorphous lumps of healthfood cake.

"Dear Beau," Evangeline said coldly. "I'm afraid I can't stay. I have the most frightful headache—"

"But it's *Sunset on the Rio Grande*—the first film Juanita and I made together. That was when we met."

"*Dear* Beau, much as I would love to see you again in the full flush of youth and virility, I simply cannot. My headache is worsening by the moment. I must get back to the flat and lie down."

"Well, then—" Beau turned to me—"*you'll* stay—?"

"Oh no," I babbled. "I feel terrible, too. That wind has brought on my neuralgia. I'm in agony—"

We were both edging towards the lift. Hugh, recognizing the inevitable, was right behind us, reaching for his car keys. "I'll tell you what—" Beau did not give up easily. "I'll set up a special screening for you in the morning. You can get a good night's sleep and see it then."

"I think not," Evangeline said firmly. "Tomorrow, I'm planning to have laryngitis."

CHAPTER 6

"Mortgaged to the hilt!" Evangeline announced with relish.

"What—everything?" I splashed more brandy into our glasses. In the background, the characters in a television serial mouthed at us; we had turned the sound off as soon as Hugh had left. "You don't mean it!"

"Cecile told me all about it. Apparently, it's been the talk of the town. There were problems with the construction workers and the building wasn't finished anywhere near on schedule. Costs ran way over budget, they had a couple of strikes, then one of the worst winters in years delayed progress still more. It seems that everything that could possibly go wrong went wrong."

"Poor Beau—but the cinema seems to be doing well."

"That won't go very far with his debts—and the running costs alone have doubled since the building opened a year ago. He'd hoped to empty half of Wardour Street into it, that's why he called it Cinema City. Along with all the office space, there are six private screening rooms and two film processing labs. He kept the Silver Screen in the Sky to run himself, thinking that the rents from the rest of the building would finance it, but the building is only half rented and he's losing money hand over fist."

"Poor Beau—that must be killing him. You two didn't waste any time in the powder room, did you?" They must have made fascinating eavesdropping if anyone else were around.

"We've barely scratched the surface." Evangeline was complacent. "I'm lunching with Cecile tomorrow—she has a late rehearsal call—and she's going to fill me in on the *real* dirt."

"How nice. You really *will* have laryngitis by the time you're through."

"You don't mind, do you? We're such old friends and we

have a lot of catching up to do. You wouldn't know most of the people, anyway."

"I don't mind," I lied calmly. "I have plans of my own for tomorrow, you needn't worry about me."

There was a sudden crash over our heads, followed by a series of heavy thumps. The ceiling shook. Jasper was either practicing a dance routine or he had started throwing the furniture around.

"And we thought *he* was the quiet one," Evangeline said bitterly.

"Oh, Tewwific! You weally mean it? You're not just being kind?"

"It's you who has been so kind," I assured her. "I really feel I'm imposing on you—"

"Oh no! No! I'd love to! Honestly!"

"Good. Get dressed then—" She was still in a surprisingly practical woollen dressing-gown, neat and serviceable but not gaudy. Presumably she only wore her bizarre costumes for public display. I tried not to think what she might consider suitable to conduct a guided tour of the High Street and surrounding district followed by lunch in one of its best restaurants. I would almost have preferred the dressing-gown.

"Ten minutes!" she promised. I didn't believe her an instant; her hair was looking almost neat, it would take at least half an hour to transform it into its usual mess.

"That's fine. I'll wait downstairs." I stepped over a cluster of dreg-stained coffee cups in the middle of the floor. "Just come down when you're ready . . ."

However, I had wronged her. It was only slightly over ten minutes later when she tapped on the door. "Good heavens, that was quick," I said.

"I did two years in Pwovincial Wep—we had to make some weally fast changes in that." She came through into the drawing-room, her clothes fluttering about her. She couldn't really have fallen into the ragbag and not quite managed to shake all the remnants off, but it certainly looked like it from where I stood. She was multi-layered with varying lengths and clashing colours. In contrast, her hair was a rigid beehive surmounted by rigid multi-coloured bees which, on closer inspection, turned out to be plastic Bulldog clips.

"I thought—" she was blissfully regardless of my reaction—"I'd show you awound Swiss Cottage, then come down to St. John's Wood High Stweet and have lunch. It has some westauwants I've always longed to twy—but they're so expensive—"

"Don't worry about that," I said briskly. "You're my guest and I'm very grateful to you for giving up your morning to show me around. After lunch, I thought I might go to Harrod's and look for a dressing-gown."

"Hawwod's . . ." she almost-echoed wistfully. "But—" she relinquished the temptation with a sigh—"I have to be at the Silver Scween at thwee . . ." She sighed again.

"Another time, perhaps." I forbore to mention that she had not been invited this time. "We could have tea there some afternoon when you don't have to work."

"Oh, Miss Dolan," she squealed. "That would be wonderful!"

"Please—" I felt guilty, seeing that I was about to start pumping the poor little wretch for all I was worth. But Evangeline had her sources of information, it was time I developed a source or two of my own. "Please, call me Trixie." Too late, I saw what I had let myself in for.

"Oh, Twixie—I'd love to!"

It's bad enough to be stuck with a name like Trixie, to begin with. Over the years, I have cheered myself with the thought that it could have been a lot worse. Hollywood never left a good plain name alone and everyone concerned got a bad attack of Terminal Twee when it came to naming new stars. The cutesy-poo awfulness of male names was bad enough, but they never rested from their excesses where the females were concerned. From Pola to Theda, through Bebe, Ginger, Osa, Lupe, Benay, Jinx, Piper and even Honey-Chile, the Hollywood Star-Making Machine did its worst, never considering what it would be like to be stuck with that name four or five decades on. Only Evangeline had beaten that rap, moving from Baby Evvie, to Eve, to Evangeline as advancing age and circumstances warranted.

"Let's get going, then," I said quickly. "I'm dying to explore the neighbourhood and get myself oriented.

Don't—" I stifled a yawn nearly as ostentatiously as Evangeline—"don't mind if I yawn a bit. My sleep was a bit disturbed last night. Tell me, is Jasper a dancer or a choreographer?"

"Gwacious no!" Gwenda laughed merrily. "Nothing so pwecawious as show business for our Jasper. He's a stockbwoker!"

Well, talk about taking candy from a baby. I ought to have been ashamed of myself, except that I learned so much. As a prime source of information, scandal and general gossip, I'd back Gwenda against Dame Cecile any day of the week.

As the characters in *Scars On Her Soul*, the gangster quickie Evangeline and I made so that the studio could cash in on the success of *Scarface*, kept saying to each other, "She sang like a canary."

"Oh, go on, Twixie—" Right now, she was egging me on. "Evewybody does it. I'll never tell. You'll never find another one like it, you know you won't."

"Well . . ." I pirouetted before the looking-glass and let myself be tempted—especially if she wouldn't tell. Tell Evangeline, that is. I wasn't worried about anyone else. I didn't know anyone else here.

We were in the Oxfam Shop in St. John's Wood High Street—a far cry from Harrod's, where I had intended to buy a new dressing-gown. The irony was that I had found the perfect one in here. I pirouetted again, the shimmering kingfisher blue brocade flowed with my every movement. It was a luxurious material and the colour was strong enough to let me stand out on my own in that red velvet drawing-room—and against Evangeline's black velvet gown. Should I be such a snob as to let it matter that it was second-hand?

"Oh, Twixie—it's *you*! You can't not buy it. You'd never forgive yourself later."

Damn it! She was right. And heaven knew, it was cheap enough. Also, it looked as though it had never been worn— or not very often. Bought and kept for best, or perhaps put away in a closet and forgotten . . .

"It isn't faded at all—" Gwenda was scrutinizing the seams with an eagle eye. "And no fwaying. It's as good as new. I weally think it *is* new. People just thwow things away sometimes because they change their minds about liking them, you know."

"Oh, all right." I gave in. "I'll take it." And may Martha never find out where I got it. If she asked, I would tell her—with perfect truth—that I had found it in a delightful little shop in St. John's Wood High Street.

However, my plans for the afternoon had to change. I couldn't go to Harrod's carrying an Oxfam bag. I would have to go back to the flat and leave my purchase there—and also dispose of the Oxfam bag before Evangeline saw it. But first . . .

"What time are you supposed to be at the cinema?"

"Cwumbs!" Gwenda looked at her watch and gasped. "I didn't wealize it was so late. I must fly!"

"You must take a taxi," I corrected. "No—no arguing." I opened my purse. "I insist. You've given up so much of your time and I've enjoyed every minute. I made you late—and this is the least I can do." I pressed a ten-pound note into her unresisting hands. "I shall want to call on your good services again—and if you don't allow me to do this, I won't feel able to."

"Oh, but I enjoyed it all, too—it was such fun. And it was such a delicious lunch—and so expensive—and the taxi won't cost nearly this much—"

"You just take it and shut up!" I folded her fingers over the banknote. "When you're starring in your first West End hit, *you* can take *me* out to an expensive lunch."

"Oh, I will, Twixie!" Her eyes shone at the thought. "I pwomise you I will."

Just as I turned the corner, a taxi drew up in front of the house. Just my luck—Evangeline was back early. I hid the Oxfam bag behind my back and approached in a sideways crablike scuttle.

Evangeline was too busy paying off the taxi to notice my approach. She was also juggling several small bags and I relaxed as I saw the name on them. I let her get inside the carriageway before I caught up with her and said, "Hello, Evangeline."

She jumped and tried to hide her own purchases behind

her back, but there were too many of them and one of the
bags slipped and fell at her feet."

"Let me—" I rubbed salt in the wound by stooping
quickly to retrieve the bag and handed it to her.

"Thank you." She took a deep breath and said quickly,
"Cecile took me to the most amusing little shop in
Kensington. I couldn't resist picking up a few things—and
it's in such a good cause. It's a charity shop, you know."

"I know." I brought my own bag out from behind my
back. "Gwenda took me to the local one. She says *everyone*
shops there and, if Dame Cecile took you, it seems to be
true."

"Snap!—as they say here." Evangeline gurgled with
amusement. "I got some books—mint condition and about
one-third of the original price—and a woollen scarf, a pair
of gloves and a bit of old jewellery, just paste, but very
sweet. What did you get?"

"Just what I wanted." We were at the door and,
unhampered by as many parcels as Evangeline, I inserted
my key in the lock. We stepped inside.

"Just wait till you see—" I broke off. We both gaped at
the scene before us.

We had caught Mick descending the stairs. Our entrance
had been too sudden to allow him time to turn and flee—or
even to think. He stood there, yellow cockscomb quivering, eyes wide with fear and despair, clutching the inert girl
in his arms and staring back at us.

"Young man—" Evangeline spoke in a voice that would
have brought Ethel Barrymore to her knees. "Is that a
body?"

CHAPTER 7

It was obvious that he would have given anything in the world to be able to say "No." With a little more nerve, he might have tried the Jimmy Durante ploy in *Jumbo* when, stopped by a policeman as he led away the stolen elephant and queried about it, he replied, "What elephant?"

But we had him dead to rights and, unfortunately, it looked as though the operative word was "dead."

"Well, don't just stand there," Evangeline said. "Come down here."

Numbly, he descended the remaining stairs. "Look," he said, his voice blank with shock, "it's not the way you think."

"Oh, isn't it?" Evangeline dropped her parcels on the hall table and moved closer to inspect the body. Unwillingly, I moved with her.

The dead girl was no one we had seen before, not that that meant much. I sometimes had the feeling that the house was full of people we had never seen. She was lying across his arms in the Scarlett O'Hara position for the staircase scene, but there were bruises on the bare dangling arms. There were more bruises on her forehead, one cheek and throat. A thin dark red thread of dried blood streaked from one corner of her mouth. She was very beautiful—and very dead.

Unnervingly, her streaked blonde hair seemed to have taken on a life of its own, it moved and quivered. Then I realized that the young man holding her was trembling violently.

"We can't stand here like this," Evangeline said. "You'd better come inside."

"No!" I recoiled instinctively. I didn't want that . . . that *thing* in our lovely little flat.

"Oh, perhaps not." Evangeline caught my thought. She

looked at Mick sharply. "Just what were you planning to do with her?"

"I thought . . . the back door . . . the garden. Leave her there. After midnight . . . when no one's around . . . move her somewhere else . . . where she could be found. Away from the house . . . away from us . . ."

"Yes," Evangeline agreed, "that might be best."

"Evangeline!" Ever since she had appeared as the feather-brained young matron with an unexplainable body on her hands in *Disposing of Larry*, she had had an unfortunate insouciance towards dead bodies. It had been remarked on unfavourably at more than one Hollywood funeral. "Why can't he just . . . just put her back where he found her?"

"No!" he choked. "Please . . . I can't! You don't know what you're asking."

It seemed reasonable enough to me, but Evangeline gave me an offended look.

"Of course you can't," she soothed the agitated young man. "Don't worry about *her*. Trixie always did see everything in black or white—and then she wonders where Martha gets it from."

"I do not—and there's no need to drag my daughter into this." That was a low blow. "And does he have to stand there holding her like that? He's giving me the creeps!"

"A good point. I suggest that you carry on with your original plan, dear boy. Go out and leave her in the garden, then come back and we'll give you a large brandy. You look as though you could use one."

"Evangeline, you're crazy!"

She paid no attention to me. She calmly gathered up her parcels and went into the flat. "I'm leaving the door open for him," she told me. "He'll be right back."

"We'll get into the most awful trouble." I followed her into the flat, still protesting. "We're foreigners here. They—they could *deport* us!"

I could see it all: the grim-visaged official stamping my passport, then the long walk between lines of stern but sympathetic Marines as I was marched up the gangplank of the waiting ship. Just like in *Canal Zone Carrie*. Only then I unmasked the Axis Agent who had stolen the secret plans

for the defence of the Canal Zone in the event of a sneak
attack which was, even then, being planned somewhere out
there in the middle of the Pacific . . .

"Don't be absurd." Evangeline spoke as though she could
read my thoughts. "Once he gets rid of the body, no one
will ever connect it with this house." We stood by the
kitchen window and watched our neighbour disappear into
the fog, still carrying the girl's body.

"Take your coat off." After a long moment, Evangeline
turned away from the window. "Let's go into the drawing-
room. We'll give that young man a few stiff drinks and then
we'll get to the bottom of this situation."

"What makes you think he'll come back?"

"Where else is there for him to go?"

"That's right—he *has* to come back. We're the only
witnesses. You know what happens to unwanted witnesses,
don't you? And *you* left the door open for him."

"Oh!" She glanced involuntarily over her shoulder. She
hadn't thought of that, although she'd been in enough of
those movies herself. They were all the rage in the 'forties
and had been having a vogue as *film noire* latterly. And
now, here we were in the stock situation: all by ourselves in
the big deserted house, thick fog outdoors and darkness
falling. Outside was a strong ruthless teenager, possibly a
psychotic, who had killed once and was disposing of the
body before returning to kill again . . .

"You and your big mouth," I said bitterly.

"Don't be silly." She had recovered her nerve—of which,
she had always had plenty. "Anyone can see he's innocent.
He'll be able to explain everything." But I noticed that she
picked up the brandy decanter and hefted it thoughtfully.

"Maybe . . ." I was more practical. I went over to the
white marble fireplace, where the fire was laid ready to be
lit, and helped myself to the brass-handled poker.

We met each other's eyes as we heard the slow footsteps
returning along the hall, and prepared to sell our lives
dearly.

We moved closer together, not quite standing back-to-
back in the swordsmen-at-bay stance. That would have
been too pointed.

Unfortunately, we were pointed enough as we were.

"Oh no!" Mick halted in the doorway, staring at the poker, at the heavy decanter gripped ready for use as a weapon. "Oh no! You don't think I—You're not afraid of me!"

To our horror, he stumbled forward, sank to his knees, buried his face in his hands and burst into tears.

It was amazing how guilty that immediately made me feel. I hadn't felt so guilty since—well, never mind. I looked at that bowed shaven head with its narrow improbable thatch and then at my poker. It would have been like bashing in an egg just as a little yellow chick was hatching out.

"It's all right, dear—" Hastily, I replaced the poker in the holder with the fire tongs and brush. "Take it easy."

"Of course we don't suspect you." Evangeline unstoppered the decanter and poured a generous measure. "Would we have asked you to come back, if we did? Here, drink this."

He groped for a glass blindly and she thrust it into his hand. He took a deep swallow and began choking.

"There—that's better." I was patting his back as much as hitting it.

"Try again," Evangeline urged. "More slowly, this time."

Between us, we got him to his feet and over to the Victorian sofa. We sat on either side of him and watched as he sniffled, took another sip of brandy and shuddered. He was so young.

"Don't you have a handkerchief?" Evangeline asked tartly.

"S-s-somewhere—" He began fumbling at the assortment of zippers decorating his outfit. There were three little zippers on each sleeve, several all over the body area and another collection up and down the legs. He explored them without success.

"Here—take this!" I thrust a slightly-used paper handkerchief at him quickly—before he unzipped the wrong compartment and embarrassed himself more than us.

"Thanks." He grabbed it and blew his nose heartily, then dabbed at his eyes. "Sorry," he said. "It—it's the shock."

"You weren't the only one to be shocked." Evangeline

refilled his glass and, this time, added glasses for ourselves.
"Suppose you tell us all about it."

This sent him back into a state of shock. His eyes glazed
and he stared off into space.

"Come along," Evangeline said sternly. "Start at the
beginning. Who is—was—this girl? Was she one of your
flatmates?"

"No. Her name was Fiona—that's all I know. She was
new. I—I don't even know what she was doing in our flat.
I—I found her in Des's bed . . . like that. Dead. I
couldn't leave her there."

Evangeline nodded, but I disagreed. "You should have
called the police. Or, at least, a doctor."

"Why? She was dead. A doctor couldn't do anything
about that."

"Then the police."

"No! Never! Don't you see—?" He was coming to life,
defending his position. "A thing like that—it could ruin us
at this stage of our careers. We'd never live it down.
There'd be all the publicity—For the rest of our lives, we'd
be known as those actors who were in that scandal about a
dead girl. Whenever we achieved anything, it would all be
dragged up again."

"Yes, I do see how you might feel that way now,"
Evangeline said, "but I think you overestimate the interest
of the public. Actually, they forget things pretty quickly."
She should know.

"Look—" I interrupted this little career advice session.
"You said that girl was in Des's bed. Where was Des?"

"He wasn't there. He went out before me this morning
and hasn't come back yet. And *she* wasn't there this
morning. I know because Des yelled to me to borrow some
hair spray and I brought it in to him. That's why I found her.
I went into his room to get it back—and there she was."

"You say you hardly knew her—"

"She was practically a stranger. I don't know what she was
even doing in our flat. I'm sure she didn't have a key."

"You've been framed!" Evangeline delivered the line she
had used to such effect in *Scars On Her Soul*.

"But why?" The idea seemed to bewilder him. "Who
would bother?"

"An enemy—?" Evangeline eyed him hopefully, but it was quite obvious that he was a bit too young to have made many enemies. He wasn't in her league. "Well, perhaps an enemy of one of the others," she conceded.

"I don't think any of us has any enemies. We've tried not to make any. We're just starting out."

It was a cogent argument. The smart ones still went by the old rule: Be nice to the people you meet on the way up; you'll meet them again on the way down.

"Are you sure about the others?" Evangeline was reluctant to give up her theory.

The front door slammed, making us all jump guiltily.

"Someone's home—" Mick tried to get to his feet, but didn't seem to be coordinating too well. "I ought to go back upstairs and—"

"And what? You're in no condition to let anyone see you," Evangeline pointed out. "They'd start asking questions—and what would you tell them?"

"What have you had to eat today?" I had a sudden qualm of my own. "Have you been drinking all that brandy on an empty stomach?"

"Er, yes," he admitted. "I'm afraid I have. That is, I had a piece of pizza about noon. It's all right," he added, as I started towards the kitchen. "I'm not hungry."

"Perhaps not, but Trixie is right. You're going to have to eat something. You have a long night ahead of you."

He finished his drink in one gulp, shuddered, and held out the glass for a refill.

"Have you . . . ?" I hesitated, but there was no delicate way to phrase it. "Have you decided what you're going to do with the body?"

Evangeline splashed more brandy into his glass.

"I've left it tied up in a plastic bin liner at the bottom of the garden. Later . . . when it's so late no one will be around . . . I'll get it and—" He paused to gulp at his drink again.

"I'll take it down and tip it into the Grand Union Canal," he went on more firmly. "The trickiest bit will be getting it across Prince Albert Road, but if I wait until two or three in the morning, it should be deserted. If there is any traffic, no one will be able to see much in this fog."

"We'll help you," Evangeline said promptly.

"We will not!" I was equally prompt. "We're five decades too old for that sort of thing." Not that we had ever indulged in running around before dawn hiding dead bodies—not unless we were following a script, that is.

"Please!" he said nervously. "I can manage it by myself. I was going to, anyway, only you came home too early and—"

"And caught you." Evangeline finished the sentence for him.

"The main thing is not to let anyone else catch you," I said. "Are you sure you'll be able to get to the canal unseen?"

"It isn't far and the fog is always worse near the water. It won't take a minute to slide her into the water. With any luck, she might float as far as Little Venice. Then no one would ever be able to trace her back here."

"With real luck, she'll sink," Evangeline said. "I don't suppose you could put some rocks in the sack to make sure . . . ?"

"Please!" He was shuddering again. "I—I couldn't untie that sack and—It was hard enough putting her into it." He was looking distinctly greenish.

"Perhaps the police won't connect her with this house." I spoke quickly to distract him. "But there may be other problems. What is Des going to say about his girlfriend disappearing?"

"Des?" Mick looked surprised. "Oh, it's nothing to do with him. She wasn't *his* girlfriend—she was Jasper's."

CHAPTER 8

"Jasper . . ." Evangeline said thoughtfully. "That wouldn't surprise me. I haven't trusted a stockbroker since the Wall Street Crash."

"All that thumping and banging around upstairs last night . . ." I was pretty thoughtful myself. "And she was covered with bruises."

"I suppose she was pregnant." Evangeline got most of her exercise these days by leaping to conclusions. "It would have been deliberate, of course. She was trying to trap him into marriage."

"I don't know. Mick said she hadn't been around very long. They hardly knew her."

"Jasper could have known her a lot longer. In any case, time isn't relevant. All it takes is one—"

"Evangeline!"

"One *night*, I was going to say." She looked at me coldly.

In the silence, the carriage clock on the mantel seemed to tick more loudly. In the distance, a church bell chimed three.

"This is ridiculous," I said. "Sitting up in the dark, waiting for Mick to come back. Why don't we put a lamp in the window? The scene lacks only that."

"You can go to bed if you're tired."

"I'm not. It's only early evening back home. My inner clock hasn't adjusted all that well yet."

"Neither has mine." She settled back in her chair. The glow from the dying fire was the only light in the room. I leaned forward and dropped a few more coals on the fire and then poked at it. I still felt a lot more comfortable with a poker in my hand.

"You don't really believe he's going to drop in and report to us on his way back?"

"It's quite possible. We're the only people he can confide

in now. We're the only ones who know what's happened."
She glanced towards the ceiling. "Except for the murderer,
of course."

"We don't know that it was murder—and we're not likely
to know until the police find the body and conduct an
autopsy."

"She didn't get into Des's bed by herself."

"You can't know that. Maybe she was friendlier with Des
than anyone suspects. She might have got into his bed
thinking she'd surprise him when he returned. Or maybe
she was just a congenital bed-hopper." Heaven knew we'd
seen enough of those in our profession.

"Slipped into his bed—and bruised herself on the
pillows?"

"Then who put her there?"

"Exactly! It was a dirty trick, planting the body on those
poor children. If they'd played it straight and called the
police, it could have ruined their lives."

"It still could, if the police find out what Mick has done.
It wouldn't do our own reputations any good, either."

"We had nothing to do with it."

"I believe it's called being an accessory after the fact," I
informed her. "And the police take a dim view of it."

"Nonsense!" The police view was a nothing compared to
Evangeline's. She rivalled Nelson at turning a blind eye to
any fact she didn't like.

"And I seem to remember something about compound-
ing a felony. And I'll bet they could cite half a dozen more
charges without pausing for breath. They'll throw the book
at us—and then they'll lock us up and throw away the key!"

"That boy has been gone too long—" Evangeline hadn't
been listening to me at all. "He should have been back by
now. Something must have gone wrong. They've caught
him!"

"In that case," I said, "they've caught us all."

The church bell had chimed four before we gave up our
vigil and went reluctantly to bed.

We slept late and awoke irritable and quarrelsome.
Especially Evangeline. What else is new?

First, the toast was too dark, then it was too light, then it was charred. (Perhaps I shouldn't have re-inserted the too light pieces and turned the control as high as it would go, but she was getting on my nerves.)

Through it all, the radio burbled inanities. At half-hourly intervals, the news was updated, with a fuller bulletin on the hour. We called a truce to hostilities at these times in order to listen avidly, but the news we were waiting to hear never materialized.

"No news is good news." I tried to cheer us both after yet another recital of radioactive leaks at a nuclear power station, the progress of a domestic seige in the suburbs, the latest Common Market scandal and the assurance that frost and fog were to be our lot for the foreseeable future.

"That's just the sort of asinine remark I'd expect *you* to make!" She was so annoyed she bit into the charred toast and then had to pretend that she had intended to. "I suppose he *did* come home safely after we'd gone to bed."

"He might have been smarter and gone somewhere else. To someone who'd give him an alibi for the whole night, no matter what time he arrived."

From overhead, there came a heavy thud.

"*He's* home, anyway," Evangeline said bitterly. "I wonder who he's murdering now."

"I hope you're not going to go around making remarks like that. It's not only slander but, remember, we aren't supposed to know that the girl is dead."

"I'm not a fool—" The telephone rang and we looked at each other hopefully.

"That may be him now." Evangeline got there first and snatched up the receiver. "Hello—?"

The line crackled briefly; she made a face at me: "Oh, good morning, Beau."

After that, the conversation got pretty one-sided. Evangeline spent most of it grimacing. Gradually, however, her expression changed and, when she replaced the receiver, she was almost in a good mood.

"That's more like it," she said. "Beau has arranged a Press Reception this afternoon. At the cinema, I'm afraid. He's out for all the publicity he can get. He'll parade us—and hope some of the glory rubs off on him."

I looked at her suspiciously. It was most unlike her to use

the word "us" in connection with any publicity that might be going. And why should she? I was just along for the ride. It was her Retrospective.

"Hugh is going to collect us in an hour and a half. . . ." Evangeline drifted back to her room. "Shall I wear the pearl chiffon or . . . ?" Her voice faded.

"You'd better wear something warm," I called to her. "He'll probably take us out on that damned roof again for the photographs."

I began to enjoy the Press Conference when I caught on to the undercurrents. Evangeline and Beau were engaged in a silent head-on clash of wills.

Beau was determined to manœuvre Evangeline into juxtaposition with the *She put the Sin in Cinema* poster. Evangeline was doing some fancy footwork to keep away from it. All around the lobby, the photographers had their cameras poised.

"Come on, Beau—" I heard one of them cheer under his breath. "Get her into frame." They wanted the shot of the two Evangelines: the young gal she had been looming over the shoulder of the stately old galleon she had become. It would be sharp, poignant—and a potential award-winner. It would also be extremely cruel.

"Beau, darling—" Evangeline wasn't playing. She side-stepped him once again as he tried to box her in. "I can't tell you how much it means to me to see your sweet face again—" Suiting action to words, she reached out to pat his face.

Several flashbulbs went off from various points around the room. It was better than nothing. The affectionate reunion of two old troupers.

"I'm only sorry dear Juanita can't be here," Evangeline cooed. "I've been so longing to see her again, face-to-face—"

Something peculiar was happening to Beau's face. It was slowly turning purple.

I caught a raised eyebrow from one cameraman and intercepted an exchange of knowing glances between two journalists. Something was happening here, but I did not possess enough information to decode the messages.

"Over here, 'Vangie—" Beau was reduced to grasping her elbow crudely and trying to drag her in front of the poster.

"Oh, Beau—" With a light laugh, Evangeline whirled skittishly and drove her other elbow into his ribs.

Beau gave a muffled *"Whoomph!"* and lost his hold on her.

"Beau, dear, I know how sinfully proud you are of your glorious roof garden. We *must* have a few pictures out there—" She caught his hand and tugged him towards the terrace door.

It was all right for her, she had taken my advice and was wearing a lilac wool dress with several layers of thermal underwear beneath it and her blonde mink cape over it. Beau was dressed for his Something-in-the-City role in a dark blue pinstripe; his navy blue cashmere topcoat had been tossed carelessly across one of the chairs.

"Come, Beau—" Evangeline gave him no chance to reach for it; no time to think of it. "Come, Beau—let's go out and *face* the music together."

An icy gust of air swept through the lobby as they went out on the roof terrace. Most of the Press Corps dashed after them, jostling each other for the most advantageous positions. Hugh, tight-lipped, brought up the rear.

I stayed where I was. Somewhere along the line, the party had stopped being polite and was deteriorating rapidly. If one of them decided to push the other off the roof, I—unlike the Press Corps—did not wish to witness it.

"Oh, Twixie—"

I had been dimly aware of Gwenda circling in the background, awaiting her opportunity. I smiled, giving her the opportunity she craved.

"Twixie, may I intwoduce Waymond Wichards—he's a mad keen fan of yours."

"How nice." I shook the proferred paw. "I didn't think anyone remembered me any more."

"Oh, Twixie," Gwenda said reproachfully, "you should know better than that."

"Yes, indeed, Miss Dolan," her young man said eagerly. "Why, *Kate of the Klondike* was screened at the NFT only a couple of seasons ago."

"Please!" I winced. "That was *not* one of my pleasantest memories."

"It wasn't?" His face lip up. I was telling him something he hadn't known, confiding in him. "Why not?"

"It was a lousy movie."

"Oh, Twixie, how can you say that? It was wonderful. You were tewwific in it." Gwenda sighed. "I'd die happy if only I could do that *gwande finale* dance woutine the way you did—"

Humming the music under her breath, she shuffled her feet awkwardly, managing to get about one move in three right. I couldn't stand it.

"No, no, Gwenda. Not like that, like this—" I showed her.

"This?" She was a quick study, she got it almost right.

"Not quite. Take it slowly . . . follow me. . . ." I led her through the steps.

"Oooooh!" She gave a squeal of delight as it began to come right.

"That's it, that's it," I encouraged her. "Now, twirl-and-kick, twirl-and-kick—"

"Oooooh!" She was getting it beautifully. In fact, she was getting beyond me. I twitched up my skirt to keep pace with her, vaguely aware that "Waymond" had taken over on the humming as we grew breathless.

"*Now* . . . a really *high* kick. That's it . . .And again . . . ." Her kick was nearly as high as mine. "Great . . ."

I thought I'd overdone it when I began to see flashing lights. Then I heard the applause as we collapsed, giggling like schoolgirls, into each other's arms, while more lights flashed.

"Well!" The temperature in the room abruptly dropped several degrees and it wasn't just because the terrace door had opened. Evangeline stepped into the lobby, her icy disapproval freezing us all.

Even the photographers who had just been snapping me looked guilty. Then one, with great presence of mind, turned swiftly and snapped Evangeline. There was a brief storm of flashing lights as the others followed suit.

Evangeline smoothed her hair into place and advanced to

the centre of the lobby, looking gratified. Behind her, Beau walked as warily as though he were tiptoeing through a minefield. The smile on his lips bore no relation to the look in his eyes. Neither had actually pushed the other off the roof, but it looked from here as though it had been a close thing.

"Trixie, dear—" Evangeline shot me a murderous look and I was suddenly glad that I wasn't standing at the edge of the roof myself. "I was just telling Beau that we can't stay. Let's face it, we're not as young as we used to be. We must go home and get our beauty sleep before the opening tomorrow."

Translation: *She* wanted to get away now and she wasn't going to leave me behind to get any publicity on my own.

"Oh, come now." With the Press looking on, Beau paraded his gallantry. "You don't look a day older—"

"Neither do you." Evangeline reached up and patted his face while the flashbulbs exploded again. "I don't know *how* you do it!"

Again, there was a subterranean tremor of amusement. I tried to pinpoint it, but couldn't. It seemed to come from several sources, yet everyone appeared occupied with their own business. Reporters were jotting down notes, cameramen took pictures. In a corner, Gwenda was earnestly imparting information to an interested young man. His pen made short strokes that might have meant he was using shorthand—or taking down a telephone number.

"My little Flower of the North!" Beau pulled her hand from his face and kissed it. This touching scene was duly recorded for posterity.

"Wicked Beau—if I took your statements at *face* value, I'd be swept off my feet. And I'm sure Juanita wouldn't approve. But we must love you and leave you. Come, Trixie—" She swept across the lobby.

"Oh, Twixie—" My little friend caught up with me as I was about to follow Evangeline into the lift. "Oh, Twixie, I was just getting it wight when all those wotten Pwess people intewwupted us. Do you think—?"

"Sure," I said recklessly. "Come down tomorrow morning—not too early—and we'll have a practice session. You have the makings of a hoofer—all you need is some practice and some of the tricks of the trade."

"Oh, thank you, Twixie—" The lift doors slid past her radiant face. Well, it was true. The kid could probably be good—if she was willing to work at it. Why shouldn't I show her the ropes? Passing along the torch to the younger generation, that was what it was supposed to be about, wasn't it? Just my tough luck that my own daughter considered acting, singing, dancing and any form of the entertainment industry as a fate worse than death. Dear Martha was never going to put herself out to entertain anybody.

"If you *must*—" Evangeline gave a long-suffering sigh— "try not to wake me. Why don't you go up to her flat? You can make all the noise you like then. It won't matter if you disturb Jasper—if his conscience lets him sleep at all."

"Evangeline—" I darted a warning glance towards Hugh, who was staring impassively at the blinking indicator lights marking our descent. It did not seem to come as any revelation to him that Jasper might be thought to have an uneasy conscience.

In fact, Hugh seemed to have something on his mind. He drove us silently and abstractedly back to the house in St. John's Wood.

Nor did I feel like indulging in snappy dialogue. The closer we got to the house, the more I kept expecting to hear police sirens. I would not have been surprised to find the place surrounded by uniformed hordes. It suddenly seemed too much to hope for that the brilliant technicians of Scotland Yard would not have traced the girl's body back to the point and place at which it had become a body.

We turned the corner into a deserted street. No police lurked behind the gate pillars as we glided up the carriageway and pulled up in front of the dark and silent house.

It should have been reassuring, but it wasn't. Something awful was going to happen. I could feel it.

"I'll let you out," Hugh said, "and then I'll go and park outside so that I won't block the drive. I won't be long. Please leave the door open for me. I want to talk to you."

"He knows!" I said as we watched him drive away.

"Knows what?" Evangeline was impatient. It was quite possible that she had forgotten all about last night. Or else had dismissed it from her mind as though it had been just a few more scenes from some long-forgotten film.

"He knows about you-know-what." I followed her up the steps and into the front hall. Not being quite sure which door Hugh had meant us to leave open, I left them both ajar as we went into our flat.

"You're not making sense, Trixie. What am I supposed to know? What do you think Hugh can know?"

"*You* know." I glanced around uneasily. Walls might not have ears, but the doors were ajar and the other occupants of the house were the type to take that as an invitation if they noticed. All we needed was to have a couple of the kids step into this.

"Oh, stop rolling your eyes like that!" Evangeline snapped. "And if you say, 'We are not alone,' I'll clout you!"

"Well, we may not be. Somebody could come in at any moment—besides Hugh, that is. And he already knows."

"Really, Trixie, I can't face much more of this—"

"And that's another thing—" Her use of the word she had been emphasizing all afternoon reminded me. "What is it with all this *face* business. You've been rubbing Beau's nose in it all day. What's the big idea?"

"You noticed, did you?" She was gratified. "And you admit there's something *you* don't know?"

"Come on, what's it all about?" I followed her into her room while we both removed our coats and automatically checked our make-up in the extravagant mirror.

"Well . . ." Evangeline added another layer of lipstick and blotted it carefully.

"Evangeline—" I threatened her with the hairbrush.

"Well, the fact is that dear Juanita hasn't been seen for the past eight years. Beau's been tellilng everyone that she's gone into retirement and can't be dragged out of the country—"

"That's what he told us."

"Yes, but the rumour is—and Cecile swears it's true— that Juanita is in hiding because she had a facelift that went wrong. Beau sent her to one of those El Cheapo Clinics and they made a mess of the operation. They were sued by some of their other clients, but of course Juanita didn't want to admit she'd been involved. Unlike dear Beau, pride meant more to her than money. The clinic was closed down—"

"I should think so!"

"But that didn't do *her* any good. *And,* to make matters worse, Beau went on to have a facelift of his own. But no cut-rate place for *him.* He wasn't saving money when it came to his *own* skin. He went to one of the best plastic surgeons in England. Juanita may never forgive him."

"You can see her point."

"They say she's so furious she won't even divorce him—just in case it might be what he wants. Still—" Evangeline placed her forefinger on a strategic spot just above one eye and pressed upwards—"you have to admit that it paid off for him. He looks ten years younger, maybe fifteen." She studied the effect in the glass.

"Just remember," I said wickedly, "if you go home looking *too* much younger, you'll lose all those lovely *grande dame* parts that have been earning you so much money."

"Hmmm . . ." She relaxed her finger and the bags fell back into their natural place beneath her eye.

"I suppose—" I half-closed my eyes to get the effect of a softened focus. "I suppose it wouldn't do any harm if we got the surgeon's name—for future reference."

"What's that?" Evangeline swung towards the door.

The sound of thundering feet shook the house. Several determined people seemed to be charging down the stairs at the same time.

"We'd better go see." I led the way with some trepidation. My feeling of impending doom had returned, although I had always thought that the British police walked with a stately tread. You live and learn.

"We'll receive them in the drawing-room." Evangeline pushed me forward as I was about to turn down the entry hall to the door. She was right, we needed all the props we could get.

They must have started from the top of the house. We had ample time to arrange ourselves in elegant postures before they arrived. Two eminently respectable elderly ladies about to be surprised by the arrival of the Law. We'd both played this scene before—give or take a few variations.

Mick burst into the room, wild-eyed, quiff quivering, as though all the hounds of hell were on his traces. "I couldn't help it," he gasped. "I thought it was all right but—"

Des pounded into the room behind him, but seemed shorter of breath. He just stood there panting and looking at us expectantly.

Ursula slid in quietly, not a hair out of place, nor was she breathless. Her eyes were shining and avid as she looked at us, then turned to watch the door.

One last set of footsteps came down the hall with the tread of doom. My heart sank. Retribution was upon us.

"Mother!" Martha marched into the room and stared at me accusingly.

"She's been here for hours—" Mick had the steam-rollered look I had learned to recognize on the faces of unwary males who had had a brief encounter with Martha. "She talked us into letting her wait upstairs. Was it all right? She said—" He looked from her to me disbelievingly. "She said you were her mother."

"That's right," I admitted grudgingly. "She's my daughter. What are you doing here, Martha?"

"You never telephoned me back," Martha accused. "I was waiting by the phone. I was worried. Frightened. What was I to think?"

"You might have thought your mother was busy living her own life," Evangeline said tartly. "She's a grown woman."

"I found her waiting on the steps," Mick said. "I didn't want to leave her out there, not knowing when you'd be back. I took her up to our place." He sounded as though he had regretted it ever since. He probably had.

"Thank you, Mick," I said comfortingly. "That was very kind of you."

"My suitcases are upstairs." Martha looked at the two boys in annoyance. "Didn't either of you bring them down?"

"We'll get them later." Des obviously didn't wish to miss a moment of this touching reunion. "Plenty of time."

"Suitcases? It sounds as though you've come prepared to stay a while." Evangeline rushed in where I dared not tread. "What hotel are you staying at?"

"Hotel?" Martha regarded her with distaste. "There's plenty of room here."

"Oh no there isn't!" I was glad Evangeline was prepared to fight it out. Left to myself, I knew I'd have caved in and offered her my bed while I slept on the chaise-longue in Evangeline's room. "You can see for yourself, your mother and I have a room each—and there's no extra space."

"Nonsense," Martha said. "This is an enormous room—and that sofa looks quite adequate."

My heart sank. This was Martha in her most mulish mood; she was digging her heels in and there would be no budging her. Still, I had to try.

"I've noticed a nice little hotel not very far away. You'd be much more comfortable there and . . ." I had to pause and get my voice under control before continuing. "And we can still see each other quite often."

Evangeline snorted.

"I'm staying here," Martha said flatly. "Whether I am comfortable or not is beside the point."

Before I could ask just *what* point she was talking about, Ursula sidled forward.

"I think I have the solution," she said. "I don't know whether you've noticed—" she glanced from Evangeline to me—"but you don't occupy the entire floor. The room opposite this one is a separate *pied-à-terre*—"

"Bed-sitter," Des muttered loudly.

"It isn't rented at the moment and I'm sure—"

"Oh, we couldn't impose like that," I said quickly, but that girl just wasn't able to take a hint.

"I'm sure," she went on smoothly, "that Jasper would be happy to let you rent it for as long as you like."

"Jasper?" Evangeline raised an eyebrow at me.

"Jasper is our landlord." That was one of the items of gossip I had almost forgotten in the press of other events. "I understand he owns this house."

"I could show it to you now," Ursula volunteered. "It's just a studio flat, but it's self-contained and very well equipped. I'm sure you'd like it."

"I'm sure of that, too," Martha said grimly. She'd sleep on the roof ridge if it meant she could keep tabs on me. "Will he accept traveller's cheques? Or I can get to a bank first thing in the morning—"

"Oh, there won't be any problem," Ursula assured her. "Not with Miss Dolan to vouch for you."

For a mad fleeting instant, I considered repudiating Martha entirely. "That woman is an impostor! I've never seen her before in my life!" But then I realized it was far too late for that. I had already admitted she was my daughter.

"Good." Martha almost smiled at Ursula. "Then perhaps you'll have my bags brought down. I'll move in immediately."

It was probably just as well that my hollow groan was lost in the burst of activity.

Ursula gestured and both Mick and Des started for the door. They narrowly avoided colliding with Hugh as he entered. There was a brisk quadrille ending abruptly as they all stopped short and waited suspiciously for someone to make the next move.

"Is this Jasper?" Martha asked.

"Oh no, dear," I said swiftly. "Let me introduce you. This is the kind man who's been looking after us so well: Hugh Carpenter. Hugh, this is my daughter, Martha."

"How do you do?" Hugh offered his hand.

"Hugh?" Martha whirled on him. "Don't you dare 'How do you do' me, you—you monster!" She dealt him a backhand blow that sent him reeling across the room.

CHAPTER 9

"All I said was, 'How do you do'—" Hugh backed away from Martha's furious advance, nursing his cheek. "What's wrong with that?"

"Don't *speak* to me!" she snarled. "Just have the decency to get out of this house—if you know what decency *is*. And never, never come near my mother again!"

"Oh no!" Suddenly I realized what this was all about. Martha, never one to give me the benefit of a moment's doubt, had believed every idiotic thing Evangeline had told her. She thought Hugh was my gigolo and had rushed to London to defend my honour—highly dubious though she had always found it.

"This—" I turned on Evangeline. "This is all your fault. I hope you're satisfied!"

Evangeline inspected her fingernails, distancing herself as far as possible from the sordid scene. But she couldn't fool me; she was delighted with the results of her nasty little joke.

"Martha—stop that!" I rounded on my daughter. "Leave that poor man alone! It's not your house, you can't order him out of it. Hugh, I apologize for my impossible child."

"I don't understand—" Hugh bleated from the corner Martha had backed him into. "What have I done? What did I say?"

"Never mind, I'll explain later." I felt a wave of colour I had not attained in more than thirty years without the generous aid of Max Factor flood my face. "Right now, I'd like to speak to Martha—privately."

"Of course, of course. I understand—" Hugh side-stepped Martha and spurted for the door. "I quite agree."

He was the only one anxious to take his departure. Mick, Des and Ursula remained riveted in their places waiting to see what new development would take place. I had the feeling that they were compiling mental notes. Some day they might be faced with a script that called for them to abandon their English reserve and let rip—they would recall this evening and be prepared.

"'I pray you'—" This was all we needed. Evangeline rose to her feet and went into her routine. "'Stand not upon the order of your going'—"

"Oh no!" Ursula cried. "You shouldn't have said that. It's the most awful bad luck. Everyone knows you should never quote from *Macbeth*!"

"You shouldn't even utter the name of *that play*—" Des had gone pale. "It's bad luck upon bad luck. The most frightful things may happen now!"

I looked at Martha. If anything worse could happen, I didn't want to know about it. Mick looked as though he might be about to faint—and that was another complication we could do without.

"Ursula—" I gave her my sweetest smile. "Perhaps you'd like to show Martha her room. Mick, Des—I believe you offered to bring down Martha's suitcases—"

I got them all moving. Reluctantly, perhaps, but moving. The show was over, so far as they were concerned. The next few scenes were going to take place in private.

"Now—" I turned to Evangeline after the room had cleared. "Now see what you've done."

I woke in the morning with a feeling of impending doom. As usual. It seemed to have taken up permanent residence at the back of my mind.

I began some deep-breathing exercises, still lying there with my eyes closed, reluctant to get up and begin the day. In retrospect, the past few days seemed happy and peaceful, untroubled by any deeper worries—

"Mother! How could you?"

Martha stood foursquare in my bedroom doorway. Was I never to have any escape from those accusing eyes?

"How could you?" she asked again.

"How did you get in here?" I had a question of my own. Very mindful of my darling daughter just across the hall, I had made damned sure there weren't any doors left ajar last night. "I *know* I locked the door."

"Ursula gave me the spare key, of course. She knew I'd want to be in and out of the flat."

"How thoughtful of her."

"Don't change the subject, Mother." Sarcasm had always been lost on Martha. "I still want to know how you could do such an awful thing."

"I've already explained—" I sighed and sat up, reaching for my new robe. There would be no more peace around here, I might as well get up and have breakfast. "Evangeline was joking. It was a very poor joke but she has a warped sense of humour—and you'd have to know Hugh to realize how funny it really was."

"Not that." Martha brandished a newspaper at me impatiently. "I mean—*this*!" She strode forward, unfurled the newspaper and waved it before my face. "How *could* you?"

"Oh!" I looked at the picture in pleased surprise. "Well, you know I've always kept limber. I found I could do it quite easily." I removed the paper from her nerveless hand and inspected it more closely.

TRIXIE SHOWS HER TRICKS the headline shouted. And there I was, out-high-kicking a girl nearly one-third of my age. Not that Gwenda was any slouch. For someone untrained, she was keeping her end up quite creditably. I nodded approval and moved on to the caption beneath the picture—which took up almost half the page, I was happy to note.

> Trixie Dolan, one of the greatest Hollywood
> Musical stars of her generation, proves that she
> still has what it takes—and plenty of it. Further-
> more, she isn't shy about passing along her tricks
> to Gwenda Parsons, who proves an apt pupil.
> Here from Hollywood for a season at the Silver
> Screen in the Sky, Trixie shows that you can't keep
> a good hoofer down—and young Gwenda isn't far
> behind. Could this be the beginning of a promis-
> ing new double act?

"I just can't understand—" Martha was close to tears— "how you can make an exhibition of yourself like that. And in a rag like that, too. Why, they have a nude on Page Three."

"In that case, I'm quite respectable. In fact, I'm a fuddy-duddy by their standards."

"It isn't funny, Mother!"

It never was with Martha. Poor girl, I had been a sore trial to her all her life. We always said the stork had dropped her down the wrong chimney: she should have gone to a Pillar-of-the-Community Churchwarden and his Social Worker wife.

"If it's such a rag," I countered, "what are *you* doing with it? I thought you'd go for a more respectable newspaper."

"I didn't buy it!" Martha was shocked at the mere idea. "I haven't even been out yet. I found it lying in the hall, just inside your door. I assumed it was yours—especially when I saw that picture."

"No, I didn't order it. I didn't even know which paper the photographer worked for." I had a pretty fair idea where the paper had come from—and she was right. I was delighted to see it, even if Martha wasn't.

"You don't care." Martha followed me around the kitchen as I filled the kettle and set it on the hob, then loaded the toaster. "You're enjoying this!"

"If you'd stayed at home where you belonged, you'd never have known about it. What the eye does not see, the heart does not grieve over. You'd have saved yourself a lot of grief."

"So now it's all *my* fault!" Martha's voice soared hysterically. "That's just like you, always twisting the truth—"

"*What* is going on here?" Evangeline came into the kitchen radiating disapproval. "*Must* you indulge in a family brawl the first thing in the morning? *Other* people are trying to sleep."

"Good morning, Evangeline." I set another place at the table. "I trust you slept well—up to now."

"Like a log—until the buzz-saw started." Evangeline glared at Martha, but refused to speak to her directly. "What's the matter with her now?" she asked me.

"Have you *seen* this?" Martha asked, unnecessarily, since it was quite obvious that Evangeline had just got up and couldn't possibly have seen a newspaper Martha had

already commandeered. "Just *look* at this!" She snatched
up the tabloid from the table and waved it at Evangeline.

"Well, let go of it, woman!" They tussled briefly for
possession of the newspaper. "How can I see it, if you won't
let go of it?"

"Don't tear it," I said. "I want it for my scrapbook."

Holding the paper at arm's length—she would never
admit she needed glasses—Evangeline frowned at the
picture, then scanned the caption.

"They've got this all wrong," Evangeline said indignantly.
"*I'm* the one having the season at the Silver Screen, not
you. They haven't mentioned me at all."

Now there were two pairs of eyes looking at me
accusingly.

"That's not my fault." I caught the toast as it popped up,
and took my cup of coffee. "You can't kick as high as I can."

I made a strategic retreat to my bedroom, closing the
door firmly behind me. They could now hold their indignation meeting. For once, they had something in common.

I dressed in my leotard—I'd only brought it along to
annoy Evangeline by wearing it while doing my exercises—
and a trouser suit, then waited until the coast was clear
before slipping upstairs. They'd never think of looking for
me there.

"Oh, cwumbs! Was I supposed to be down there
alweady? I'm so sowwy. I'll come wight along—"

"No, no, it's all right." I slid past her into the room. "I just
had second thoughts. It occurred to me that it would be
better to do our practice up here. Not so much furniture—
and easier to roll the rugs back. If that's all right with you?"

"Oh yes, anything you say." She was still in her warm
woolly bathrobe. "It's so kind of you—"

"Not at all." I stepped over the cluster of coffee mugs in
the middle of the floor. Were they the same mugs or had
they been refilled several times since I had last seen them?
"I might as well do something useful while I'm here."

"Would you like a cup of coffee?" Gwenda bent and
swooped up the mugs. "Some toast? Anything?"

"No, thank you, I've just had breakfast." I caught a

movement out of the corner of my eye and turned to catch a sleek dark head trying to dodge out of sight.

"Come in," I called.

"You know Ursula," Gwenda said, "but I don't think you've met Anni. She was out when you awwived."

"Hello, Anni." I nodded coldly to Ursula. Anyone who went around giving out keys to my flat was not going to lead my Popularity Parade. "Hello, Des—" I waited, but no one else came through the doorway. "What, no Mick?"

"He's sleeping," Des said. "At least, I hope he is. I heard him pacing the floor until all hours. He hasn't been sleeping well lately."

I don't suppose he was. The memory of his grim task was not one he would be able to shrug off lightly.

"Oh, please—" Ursula stepped forward, clasping her hands in a parody of one of Gwenda's gestures. "Miss Dolan, Gwenda told us you're going to give her a tap-dancing lesson. Please, please, may we watch?"

"It's your flat," I said ungraciously. "If Gwenda doesn't mind, I don't."

"Oh, thank you—"

"We're going to need some space cleared—and those rugs rolled up." I kicked at a corner of a runner intruding into the room.

"We'll do that." Des bent and began rolling back the runner. Ursula effortlessly pushed a large armchair back against the wall. Anni smiled at me vaguely and let the other two do the work.

"What kind of music, Twixie?" Gwenda was back, offering a selection of tapes. "I thought p'waps this one—" She held out a cassette titled *The 'Thirties Song and Dance*.

"That will do," I agreed. Just about anything would do except rock and its later variations.

"Now!" I started Gwenda off with some basic steps as the music swung out. She was enthusiastic and eager to learn. As the lesson proceeded, it dawned upon me that she wasn't the only one.

Over on the sidelines, a fair amount of audience participation was going on. Anni and Ursula were attempting to copy the steps, even Des was furtively shuffling his feet, frowning with concentration. I might have known it.

"Oh, all right!" I gave up. "Get over here into line—all of you. You can't see what you should be doing from over there."

Gwenda was unperturbed as they dashed to line up on either side of her. She was right. They hadn't her aptitude, but knowing a good basic routine would never come amiss for any of them.

I put them through their paces until we were all limp and sweating. By the end of the session, I was aware of a growing uneasiness which finally crystallized into coherent thought:

Where was Mick? Why hadn't he given up his attempt to sleep and come out to join us? He couldn't still be sleeping through all this racket.

We were making enough noise to wake the dead.

"There have been three telephone calls this morning," Evangeline said severely when I returned. "*All* for you."

"How nice? Did they leave any messages?"

"Two were from newspapers who wanted interviews—with photos. The third said he'd ring back." She gave me a tight smile and added casually, "Martha told the newspapers that you wouldn't give interviews and were not available for photographs."

"Oh, she did, did she?" I had been feeling tired after my unaccustomed workout, now the surge of adrenalin snapped me to attention, ready to fight the world. "Where *is* Martha?"

"I sent her out sightseeing. She was getting on my nerves."

"Just as well." I did some deep breathing, trying to cool my temper. "I might have killed her."

"That would be too much to hope for. You should have dealt more firmly with that girl from the beginning. She has no right to rule your life the way she does."

"She doesn't, really. Not when I'm around."

"Precisely. And how many offers do you think she may have refused on your behalf when you weren't around to know what she was doing? It came as quite a revelation to me, I can tell you."

It was a revelation to me, too, but I wasn't going to let

her see that. But, once roused, the suspicion was hard to quell. Thinking back, I realized that my career had slowly begun to slip just about the time Martha graduated from college and came home to live with me.

There was that TV series I had been approached about and then heard no more—until it went on with someone else in the role. Could Martha have intercepted a vital telephone call and told them I'd lost interest? And how about that tantalizing whisper that there might be a lead in a Road Company revival of *Broadway Follies*? That, too, had come to nothing—at least, so far as I was concerned. Was it possible that I had not so much chosen retirement as had it forced upon me?

"Let's go out to lunch." Evangeline glanced at her watch.

"I'm not hungry." I had shared frozen pizzas and coffee with the kids after the lesson. It had taken me back more years than I cared to count to be sharing a scratch meal, laughs, dreams and theatre gossip with a group of young hopefuls.

And that was another grievance against Martha: if she had minded her own business instead of mine, got married and produced a few heirs, I'd have a gang of grandchildren to frolic with and teach now. The pizza was awful, of course, but a couple of antacid tablets would put me right.

"That's not the point," Evangeline said. "If we go out to lunch now, we can stay away until it's time to come back and get dressed for the Opening. We'll miss Martha altogether, if we can time it right."

Some time during that day, the body was discovered. The Stop Press column of the early edition carried the item. An unidentified woman found in the Grand Union Canal. The later editions, or maybe the morning papers, might carry a fuller story. Or maybe they wouldn't. The clear implication was that suicide was suspected.

I pointed it out to Evangeline and gave her the newspaper, but we were in a taxi on our way home and could not discuss it. We exchanged glances and nods.

I couldn't say anything, but I knew we weren't nodding about the same things. Evangeline was nodding a cool professional appreciation of a job well done; the body

disposed of without fuss and discovered far from where it
could rebound on any of us.

I was just relieved that it had been found. I hadn't liked
to think of the poor young thing floating in the cold water,
shrouded by the damp heavy fog.

The fog was heavier than ever now and the taxi was just
crawling along. We were going to be late. If only, I thought
wistfully, the fog had been this bad yesterday, perhaps
Martha's plane wouldn't have been able to land and would
have been diverted to an airport on the Continent.

"Here we are. Don't bother driving up to the house,"
Evangeline said to the bemused driver, who was not even
aware that we had reached our destination, far less that
there was a driveway concealed somewhere behind the fog.
"We'll get out here."

She got out and disappeared into the mists, leaving me to
pay the driver. I knew what that meant: she had slipped
into her most regal mood. Royalty doesn't carry cash. She
was getting ready to Queen it at the Opening tonight.

Martha was still nursing her grievances when I got in,
but I gave her short shrift.

One *prima donna* at a time was enough.

CHAPTER 10

All things considered, it was amazing how well *Revenge of the White Squaw* had stood up against the passage of time.

There had also been some magnificent restoration work done on it. Ursula had told me this morning, with justifiable pride, the bits to look out for; otherwise I would never have guessed that the archive restorers and not the scriptwriter or director had been responsible for some of the linking scenes. The big dramatic scenes had fortunately survived almost intact—and how much power they had, even today.

The audience was swept by emotion as the young Evangeline, carrying her baby son, fled from the pursuing party of Indians on the War Path. They groaned as she was caught, gasped at the audacity of the implied mass-rape, and handkerchiefs began to flutter as she became a slave to the squaws of the tribe and plaything of the braves. Then came the moment when she held her dead son in her arms and gave that famous silent scream.

There wasn't a dry eye in the house—mine included. We needed the cut to the Army headquarters as the news reached them of her capture and they mounted a rescue mission to pull ourselves together after such intensity of emotion and to brace ourselves for what was still to come: The Revenge.

The moon rose over the desert and a silhouette of a howling coyote filled the screen. The Indian camp was silent, shadowed, then something stirred. Evangeline, tethered to a stake beyond the dying campfire, slowly sat up and pulled the knife she had stolen earlier from beneath her concealing skirt. She cut the rawhide thong tethering her and crept into the tepee where the Chief slept.

He stirred. She froze. He turned over and was quiet again. She waited, then moved forward, hatred blazing in

REEL MURDER   79

her eyes, knife held high. He sensed another presence, he frowned in his sleep, his eyelids flickered and opened.

Too late. Evangeline struck. He died without making a sound. She stood looking down at him, then she withdrew the knife and leaned over the body. Working swiftly, she made the V-shaped incision where the scalplock sprang back from the forehead, then slashed along the sides of the scalplock. Hands slippery with blood, she grasped the forehead flap and tore with all her might.

The audience screamed. She straightened triumphantly, holding aloft the bleeding trophy. The White Squaw had taken her first scalp.

But not her last. As the moon faded, the coyote slunk away, the campfire went out, Evangeline slipped from tepee to tepee, her trail marked by the blood dripping from the scalps hanging from her waist.

"Came the dawn . . ." The titles resumed, no one had missed them. Another stock silhouette, this time of a crowing cock. The sky lightened, the Indian camp began stirring. The old squaws rose, yawning, and began to make up the campfire, to prepare breakfast for the braves. Then a squaw ran out from one tepee, screaming. The others gathered round her, listening with disbelief, then pushed her aside to enter the tepee.

They gazed down incredulously at the butchered brave, saw the drops of blood leading from the tepee and followed them. From tepee to tepee, with increasing despair and horror.

"The Chief. Who will dare to tell the Chief."

Crowding together, arguing and frightened, they approached the Chief's tepee, but . . . what's this? Drops of blood are here, too. It can't be! It is!

A shout from a squaw who had stayed behind to build up the campfire. She gestures, holding up the rawhide thong where the captive had cut herself free from the stake. Now *they* are out for revenge. They begin to search for the White Squaw.

"Meanwhile . . ." The cavalry mounted at dawn and began the ride to the rescue. Grim-faced heroic soldiers ride across the barren landscape . . . Intercut with shots of the angry squaws coming closer to Evangeline's hiding place . . . Back to the cavalry . . . back to Evangeline,

prepared to sell her life dearly as the squaws burst into her refuge . . . Back to the cavalry . . . will they be in time?

What else? Only a certain amount of grim reality was permitted in those days. The heroine had to survive to be rescued by the handsome hero. Still draped in scalps, Evangeline swooned into Beauregard Sylvester's manly arms.

Evangeline got a standing ovation, of course.

The house lights went up and Beau led her onstage, holding up his hand to try to quiet the hysterical audience.

"I think you'll all agree," he said, "that we've got the Evangeline Sinclair Season off to a rousing start."

After another minor uproar, he was allowed to continue with his speech. He must have written it himself, the cinema began clearing while he was still speaking. Unfortunately, I had to remain to the end.

Most of the audience dispersed then and the crowd remaining had invitation cards to the Champagne Reception which followed. I cheered up considerably then and it wasn't just the champagne.

There were a lot of familiar faces around. Familiar from stage and screen, even though I hadn't met many of them personally. Quite a few had seen my photograph in the morning papers, however, and I soon had a circle surrounding me, smaller but more select than the crowd besieging Evangeline.

The usherettes were serving drinks and canapés and Gwenda took it upon herself to see that my group was kept well supplied. Naturally, some of them recognized her as the pupil in the photograph and, equally naturally, she was delighted. It all got very convivial and I found myself having the best time I had had since we landed.

The same couldn't be said for some of the others. Over in one corner, Hugh was morosely nursing his one measly glass of champagne since he was driving us back. Martha was mooching around by herself in another corner, sulking. The house had been sold out, not even standing room, and she had not been able to get in to the film. She had been

given a ticket to the reception, but that wasn't good enough
for Martha. I'd never hear the end of her complaints.

Gwenda refilled my glass and I stopped fretting. Let's
face it, Martha would enjoy having a legitimate grievance
more than she would have enjoyed the movie. Too bad
about her.

The next time I noticed her, she had gravitated to Hugh's
corner and they were both talking earnestly. From the
expressions on their faces, they were both apologizing.
Fine, that could keep them gainfully occupied for hours.

As I watched, a tray of drinks was carried past them and
Hugh absently reached out and took another glass of
champagne. Even better. He looked as though he could use
some relaxation. It couldn't be an easy life, being a go-fer
and I'd bet Beau ran him right down into the ground. We
could always take a taxi home.

Someone raised a hand to me in farewell as he slipped
out into the lift. I waved back automatically, then blinked as
I realized who it had been. Earlier, I had seen Des's multi-
coloured spikes bobbing about as he mingled with the
crowd; now his hair was back to its normal shade, lying flat
and rather damp. He was obviously on his way to work
somewhere.

I didn't see any of the other kids from the flat-share
there. Of course, Ursula had worked on restoring the film,
she would have seen enough of it. Anni was still an
unknown quantity, neither her absence nor her presence
would have been surprising.

It was Mick I was worried about. Even if he'd managed
to sleep all day to compensate for his sleepless nights, he
should have been stirring by now. But he wouldn't necessarily show up here. After his nightmare experience with
the girl's body, he wouldn't want to be harrowed further. He
didn't need to add grisly filmatic scenes to his memory
bank; his real-life experiences were grisly enough.

Jasper was quite ostentatiously present, however. He
appeared to be the sole escort for at least three beautiful
girls. As I watched, another one came up and joined them.
He obviously was not pining for the girlfriend who had
disappeared; if, indeed, he had even noticed her absence.

Or if, as Evangeline believed, he had killed the girl

himself, his conscience obviously wasn't troubling him in any way.

Or was it? Despite the fact that the night was still fairly young, he seemed to need the assistance of the girls on either side of him to keep him upright—which didn't stop him from commandeering a fresh tray of drinks as they went past. It was going to take a whole fleet of taxis to get us all back to the house tonight.

One of the cinema flunkies brought over someone he introduced to me as a Diary snoop just then. (He'd been helping himself rather lavishly to the drinks, too.)

All right, I'll admit it, I was knocking back my share. Otherwise, I might have been more discreet. I had had warnings about the English gossip writers and their headlines, but I was caught off-guard.

"How does it feel to be a piece of living history?" he asked. What kind of a question is that?

"You'd better ask Evangeline," I said. "She's a lot more historic than I am."

His eyes lit up and, too late, I saw the trap I had fallen into. Fallen? I'd taken a head-first dive into it. And, come morning and the big black headline, Martha would be "*How could you*-ing" at me again. She was here—why wasn't she stopping me from making quotable catty remarks instead of brow-beating Hugh in corners?

"Excuse me," I said icily, "I must go and speak to my—to someone."

When I looked back over my shoulder, I saw that he was heading straight for Evangeline. Just as I'd thought, he was determined to stir up trouble.

Martha and Hugh were not in the corner when I reached it, but they had been there only a moment ago. I had distinctly seen them both take fresh drinks and give every indication of settling down for the evening. Apparently, they weren't going to settle here.

Another survey of the lobby proved that Martha and Hugh were not in sight and that Evangeline was snorting fire at the gossip columnist. Her head reared back and her eyes flashed flames as she looked around the room. I knew who she was looking for.

Fortunately, the lift doors opened just then and dis-

gorged a few late-comers to the party. I dodged behind
them and into the lift. I'd go home by myself and make sure
that I was asleep before anyone else got back. By tomorrow,
Evangeline would have cooled off.

I don't like taking sleeping pills, but two of them seemed
a strategic necessity that night. I left the bottle ostentatiously displayed on my night table and everyone must
have taken the hint. I slept without disturbance until the
morning.

I did not wake refreshed. Unremembered nightmares
clung like cobwebs as I drifted up towards consciousness.
In fact, I woke to a fresh nightmare. Someone was trying to
strangle me.

I was fighting for breath. My nostrils were pinched
together, my chin was forced down, holding my mouth
open and someone was blocking my breathing and blowing
into my throat. I hit out feebly.

"She's coming wound," a voice shrilled. "Keep going,
Des. She's coming wound!"

Another blast of second-hand air was forced into my
lungs.

"Stop that!" I flailed feebly at the head so uncomfortably
close to mine. "What do you think you're doing?"

"He's giving you the Kiss of Life. Oh, Twixie, why did
you do it?"

"Kiss of—" That snapped me back to full wakefulness. I
sat up and pushed Des away. "Do what? What are you
talking about?"

"There," Des said. "I told you it was an accident. She
woke up in the middle of the night, forgot she'd taken any
and took some more. It happens all the time."

"Now see here—" It was beginning to make faint sense.
"This is ridiculous. You're over-reacting to a perfectly
normal—" Automatically, I looked at the bedside table. The
bottle of sleeping pills lay on its side.

It was empty.

"No," I said. "That isn't possible. I only took two. There
was almost a full bottle left."

"You see? You don't wemember."

"There's nothing to remember! Look at me—" I leaped

out of bed and stood before them. "Do I look as though I'd taken an overdose?"

"Put your wobe on before you catch pneumonia." Gwenda held it for me. "You *do* seem all wight," she admitted.

"Of course I am!" There was nothing like a surge of fury to get the adrenalin flowing and all the little grey cells ticking over. "Someone emptied that pill bottle while I was asleep. Where's Martha?"

"We sent her into the kitchen to make coffee. She was too distwaught to be helpful in here."

"I'll bet," I said grimly. Martha knew what my mood would be when I awoke to find myself worked over by a couple of enthusiastic would-be rescuers who had misread the situation because she had confiscated the remainder of my sleeping pills.

"And we've been twying to keep it quiet. Evangeline is still asleep and we don't want to distuwb her."

"Pity." I couldn't hold back a grin. "You're sure she's having a nice natural sleep? Maybe she helped herself to the rest of my sleeping pills. You wouldn't like to go in and wake her up the way you woke me? Go on—make her day!"

"Oh, Twixie, I'm sowwy—"

"We thought we were doing the right thing," Des defended. "How were we to know? Martha came rushing upstairs, hysterical—"

"Martha got you down here?"

"She found you. She thought . . . She was tewwified. Who wouldn't be? But she didn't want any publicity, so she wushed to us for help, to see what we could do before she called a doctor."

"I see." That sounded like Martha, all right. Except that, in this instance, she was right. No one needs that kind of publicity. Even when it was discovered to be all a mistake, some of the mud would stick. People always like to believe the worst.

"Here's the coffee—" Ursula came into the room carrying a tray. "Oh, good, she's better."

"There was nothing wrong with me—"

"Mother!" Oh fine, that was all I needed. Martha rushed

into the room. "Mother, why did you do it? Where have I failed you?"

"It's all wight—she didn't do it."

"It was all a mistake—"

The voices rose in frantic babble. I sat down on the edge of the bed and reached for the coffee Ursula had set on the bedside table. The empty bottle had been pushed aside by the tray and one more little nudge would send it flying off the table. I looked at it thoughtfully, realizing I wasn't quite as awake as I thought I was. There was a nagging idea trying to come through—

"And *now* what is going on?" Evangeline's voice, trained to reach the farthest corner of the second balcony in the days before everybody pranced around wearing throat mikes, soared effortlessly over the others, silencing them abruptly.

"Sleep is impossible in this house!" she declaimed.

"You can say that again," I muttered.

"Trixie." Evangeline's icy look let me know that I had not been forgiven for last night's *faux pas*. "Can you explain all this hubbub?"

"No," I said. I took another sip of coffee. I wasn't even going to try. "I don't know anything about it. I was sleeping—or trying to."

"That was the twouble—" Gwenda leaped into the breach. "We thought—"

"You mean Martha thought," Ursula corrected. "We didn't know anything about it until she came running upstairs to get us."

"Ah, yes . . ." Evangeline gave a long-suffering sigh. "Martha. I might have known it would come down to Martha."

"Martha," I echoed thoughtfully. "Martha, why don't you be a good girl and go and bring me back my sleeping pills?" Even as I spoke, the flaw in my reasoning became clear to me: if Martha had taken away the pills, the empty bottle would not have upset her.

"I haven't got them," Martha said. "Why do you always accuse me of everything?"

Because you're usually responsible. I bit back the answer and tried for a softer one.

"I was only asking. You didn't take them?"

"Certainly not! Why would I do a thing like that?"

"Then where are they? I didn't take them, either."

"Are you sure?" Martha eyed me suspiciously. "All we have is your word for that—" Her voice began rising. "You might just be having a momentary rally before you collapse. I think you ought to have your stomach pumped!"

"Pull yourself together, Martha!" Evangeline's tone was a slap in the face. "You're hysterical! Stupid and hysterical! I'd suggest you go and take a walk in the fresh air to clear your brain and regain control of yourself."

"There isn't any fresh air." Martha's voice was sulky. "There's nothing but fog out there."

"Whatever there is, it can only improve you." Evangeline took her elbow and marched her firmly towards the back door. "Walk to the end of the garden and back six times—taking a deep breath at every step. It will do you a world of good."

It wouldn't do us any harm, either, to be rid of all that hysteria and pulsating emotion. Martha was one of the most exhausting people I knew.

We heard the back door slam, then Evangeline came back into the room and looked at me sternly. "That woman is in a bad way," she said. "You should have sent her to a psychiatrist long ago."

"I did," I said, "but she bit him."

"I thought that was the dentist."

"She bit him, too."

Martha had only been gone a few moments when she suddenly began screaming.

CHAPTER 11

The screams were loud, insistent, bloodcurdling. We erupted from the house and charged down the garden path in a body. The fog was thick, damp and impenetrable. We could not see two feet in front of us.

Only the high-pitched, agonized shrieks kept us on course. She was at the very end of the path, hand covering her face, shutting out something that lay behind the fog.

"Martha—" I caught one arm and pulled her hand away. "What is it? What's the matter?"

"Have a thought for the neighbours, woman!" Evangeline snapped. "If you keep on like this, they'll call the police—and I won't blame them. You're disturbing the peace."

"There—" Martha gasped. "It's— He's—" She pointed into the fog with a shaking hand. "On the garden bench!"

"I'll stay with Martha," Ursula volunteered nobly, sounding a little sick. "You go ahead."

We approached the bench cautiously. As we drew nearer, we could see the dark motionless figure slumped there.

For an instant, I could have sworn my heart stopped. That was where Mick had left Fiona's body through that long night. But it couldn't be. She couldn't have come back. They had found her body in the canal. This was someone else. This was—I stepped forward for a closer look.

"Mick!" Gwenda indentified the body a split-second ahead of me. "It's Mick!"

He's dyed his hair red, I thought inconsequentially. *And he's flattened it down. How odd. I wonder why he did that.*

My mind refused to let me realize what I was looking at.

"Good God!" Evangeline was tougher. She faced the body unflinchingly and pronounced her verdict. "The boy's been scalped!"

* * *

Whatever you do, don't ever ask Evangeline if she doesn't think the English police are wonderful.

By the same token, if you value your skin, you won't inquire of Detective-Superintendent. Heyhoe if he asked Evangeline Sinclair for an autographed photograph as a souvenir.

It was hate at first sight.

He wasn't very fond of the rest of us, either.

It didn't help that we all got off on the wrong foot—or collective feet. That was Evangeline's fault. She had brought the kids into the drawing-room and dispensed generous libations against shock. None of us had had much in the way of breakfast, the kids weren't used to drinks of that strength and Evangeline kept the glasses topped up. By the time the police arrived, we were feeling no pain.

The pain was all Detective-Superintendent Heyhoe's.

"Not interrupting a party, are we?" He looked around disapprovingly.

Des had gone upstairs and brought down his clarinet. He hadn't been playing it, he was just clinging to it as to a life raft, but Detective-Superintendent Heyhoe wasn't to know that.

Gwenda and Ursula were off in a corner dulling their reactions by trying to pretend that it was important that they master the dance steps I had taught them.

Martha was sprawled inelegantly on the sofa. Of us all, she was the most sober, but was projecting an image of utter abandon, if not depravity. She looked like the morning after the orgy. Her skirt was awry, disclosing far more of her thighs than she would ordinarily have allowed, but she was past caring. She lay motionless, eyes closed, mouth slightly open.

Detective-Superintendent Heyhoe strode over and stood looking down at her sombrely for a moment, then raised his head. "When did you discover the body?" he asked.

Someone giggled from the corner.

"That isn't the corpse—" Again, I considered disowning her, but I knew it wouldn't work. "That's my daughter, Martha. She discovered the body.

"Martha, sit up! The police are here."

"About time, too." Martha opened her eyes and glared

at the Detective-Superintendent. "What took you so long?" She tugged down her skirt with the clear implication that he had been taking advantage of the view.

A younger policeman was standing at a respectful distance, his carefully expressionless face betraying that he was enjoying his superior's discomfiture all too much.

"The body is at the bottom of the garden," Evangeline said.

Detective-Superintendent Heyhoe looked at her suspiciously and I remembered what else was supposed to be at the bottom of the garden.

"It's true," I told him. "Shouldn't you go out there and inspect it?"

"All in good time, madam." He glared at the three of us and then transferred his glare to the rest of the audience. "Isn't anyone here English?" he demanded.

The kids crowded forward and I could see him regretting his question.

"We are." Gwenda took the lead, her hair had shaken loose from half its bulldog clips while she danced. "And we're so glad that you've come to help us in this time of tewwweible, tewwweible twagedy."

Detective-Superintendent Heyhoe closed his eyes briefly and visibly stiffened his upper lip.

"We're ever so near the Zoo," Ursula said helpfully. "Have you checked to make sure that none of the wild animals have escaped? The way poor Mick was mutilated—" She could not continue and turned away.

"You knew the deceased?" Detective-Superintendent Heyhoe seized on the least emotive opening in her speech.

"We all did," Des answered. "We live in this house. Mick is—was—part of our flat-share."

"See here, Heigh-Ho—" Evangeline poured more Scotch into Ursula's glass. "Why don't you go and solve your case and stop harassing these poor children?"

"That's Heyhoe, madam." He gazed at her with disfavour. "And what might your name be?"

"I—" she drew herself up—"am Evangeline Sinclair."

"Indeed." He gave no sign of recognition. "Would that be Miss or Mrs.?"

"Mzzzzz," Evangeline snarled.

The name may have meant nothing to Detective-Superintendent Heyhoe, but his sidekick quivered and went on point like a bird dog flushing a covey of particularly fine pheasants. His eyes lit up and he all but wagged his tail.

"Evangeline Sinclair," he breathed. "*The* Evangeline Sinclair! Forgive me for not recognizing you at once, but I never dreamed we'd meet under these circumstances. I'd read you were in town."

"Dear Boy—" Evangeline gave him her most gracious smile. "How nice to know that the Arts are not unappreciated by *some* members of the constabulary. You are—?"

"Detective-Sergeant Julian Singer." He almost bowed and, still bent, swivelled to include me. "And *you*—" he breathed—"must be Trixie Dolan."

Say what you will, there is nothing like a nice obsequious minion for restoring one's *amour propre*. I beamed at him as fatuously as Evangeline. "I'm very pleased to meet you, Sergeant Singer. Do I gather you're a film buff?"

"Completely, utterly, hopelessly. This is a great moment in my life. I never dared hope I'd have the honour—"

Detective-Superintendent Heyhoe cleared his throat meaningfully and his sergeant fell silent abruptly.

"Quite finished, are we?" he asked nastily. "I wouldn't like to cut short a meeting of the fan club, but we *do* have a murder to investigate."

The statement was punctuated by the slamming of car doors in the carriageway outside. There was something businesslike and definitive about that series of small explosions; the rest of the technical crew had arrived, the investigation was about to begin.

I noticed that the doorbell didn't ring. That would mean that they had left another policeman guarding the door to let in his colleagues. We heard the heavy tramping of innumerable feet marching down the hallway to the back door. There would be a doctor among them to certify the death, a photographer to record it, various specialists to disperse themselves around the garden hunting for footprints, fingerprints, bloodstains—there would be plenty of those . . .

I began to feel faint and sank down on the sofa, just

missing Martha's feet. She swung herself into an upright
position and put a protective arm around my shoulders.

"We demand a lawyer," Martha snapped at the senior
officer. "I believe we are allowed one. We refuse to say
anything more until we have a lawyer present."

"Certainly, madam." Detective-Superintendent Heyhoe
seemed to be trying not to grind his teeth. "That is your
right. You may telephone your legal representative now."

"Oh—" The wind went out of Martha's sails. She had no
more idea of who to call than any of us. "Yes—" She looked
around distractedly.

"Oh, cwumbs!" Gwenda said. "We'd better start by
calling Hugh."

Hugh, Beauregard and Jasper arrived within minutes of
each other, uttered a few meaningless noises at us and went
to join the police in the garden. If there was a lawyer
anywhere in attendance, I didn't see him.

I had half-expected the Press to be hot on their heels, but
it appeared that we were to be spared that for a while
longer. Evidently no one had yet connected the event that
had happened with the visitors in the house. I wondered
how much longer that kind of luck could last.

Not much longer. The young detective-sergeant popped
his head round the door to goggle incredulously at Evangeline for a moment. It was clear that he had just come from
viewing the body. What a pity that we'd had to get a film
buff in the investigating squad. On the other hand, there
were bound to be some reviews of last night's shindig in the
morning papers, so someone would be putting two and two
together and getting five any minute now.

"Did anyone get any newspapers this morning?" Evangeline seemed to be following my train of thought.

"Cwumbs, I forgot! I was so fwightened when I thought
that Twixie had—"

"I think we'll forget all about that little episode, dear,"
Evangeline said firmly. "It doesn't add anything to the
situation we have here now."

"Oh, wight. I'll go and get the papers—" Gwenda started
for the door.

"Perhaps it might be a good idea if Martha went,"

Evangeline suggested. "I'm sure she could do with a bit of air and a nice little walk to calm her down."

"I am perfectly calm!" Martha snapped. "You just want to get rid of me!"

"They probably wouldn't let any of us leave, anyway," I said regretfully. "Why don't we just telephone the shop and see if they'll deliver?"

"I'll do it." Ursula rushed for the telephone, obviously delighted to have something to occupy her.

In fact, we could all do with something to occupy our minds and keep them from dwelling on the macabre figure slumped on the garden bench, blood oozing from his ripped scalp. It must be even worse for the kids; we had just met him, but he was a friend of theirs. They were putting up a brave front, but there were moments when tears glistened in their eyes. They had probably never experienced death before, far less a violent death with malicious disfigurement. They were so young, so vulnerable; my heart ached for them.

My heart ached for Mick, too. This was what he had tried to spare them. Now he was the reason that they were in the midst of a police investigation. Pretty soon, the police were going to come back and start asking why anyone should have wanted to murder him.

That meant that Evangeline and I had better think up some fairly snappy reasons for having helped Mick conceal that earlier death. I had the nasty feeling that the police weren't going to like any explanation we could give them. As I had pointed out to Evangeline at the time, we were several kinds of accessory after the fact and the police weren't going to be happy about it.

Where was that lawyer? My heart had stopped aching abruptly and my head had begun. We were in big trouble.

Not that it seemed to bother Evangeline. It was quite possible that she had forgotten the earlier incident, that it had sunk to the bottom of her consciousness where it lay among dozens of similar scenes she had played when the cameras were turning. The fact that I had spent a good many years as an actress myself never blinded me to the realization that our grasp of reality was sometimes tenuous.

At the moment, she was more concerned with needling

Martha. And Martha, of course, kept allowing herself to be needled. If she would only ignore it, Evangeline would soon stop her silly little game. The sound of their bickering was beginning to grate on my nerves.

So were the heads that popped round the door to survey us and then withdrew quickly again. They were starting to inspire a strong desire to hurl an ashtray at the next one to see if I could still hit a moving target.

Finally, a familiar face dithered there—and the impulse to hurl something intensified.

"Come in, Hugh," Martha said. "And, for heaven's sake, tell us what's going on out there."

"Yes, well . . ." Hugh sidled into the room and stood at the back of the chair Martha now occupied, giving the strong impression that he was hiding behind her skirts. "Well, the police have been very busy. Measuring, photographing, all that sort of thing. I think they're just about finished now. I mean, they're moving Mick— His body—"

I realized that Hugh was as shocked and stunned as the kids. He had known Mick, too. The realization even seemed to reach Martha, she twisted in her chair to look up at him anxiously.

"Yes . . ." he said vaguely, as though someone had asked a question. "Well, they're talking to Jasper now. They want to talk to everyone who lives in the house."

"Do they?" Ursula looked around the room, her eyes bright and sharp. "They'll be lucky! Where's Anni?"

"Cwumbs! That's wight." There was no sharpness in Gwenda's eyes, only anxiety, as she looked around. "I haven't seen her since yesterday. Where is she?"

"Either she didn't come home last night—" Ursula spelled out the possibilities, just in case we had missed them. "Or else she left early this morning—very early."

"I don't think we should jump to any hasty conclusions." Hugh immediately made matters worse. "There's probably a very good explanation if we happened to know it."

"Does she usually stay away all night?" I asked quickly.

"Er . . ." Des was trying not to shock the elderly ladies—bless him! "Well, it wouldn't be the first time."

So much for Anni.

"And . . ." Evangeline nodded, as though it had been

no more than she had expected. "And was she a *particular* friend of Mick's?"

"Er . . ." Des was looking very unhappy. "They were rather good friends, yes. I think you could say that."

"Oh, Des!" Ursula said impatiently. "They were living in the same room and you know it."

"Er . . . yes . . . but . . ." He wriggled uncomfortably.

"*And* they had a double bed in there," Ursula persisted relentlessly. "Don't be so mealy-mouthed." She had a more realistic assessment of our shock quotient than he had.

"I think what Des is twying to say is that they haven't been getting along at all well lately. They've spent as much time fighting as—oh, cwumbs!" Gwenda clapped her hand over her mouth as the implication struck her.

"But she couldn't have," Des protested. "Not Anni."

"Someone did," Hugh said sombrely.

Not surprisingly, this remark threw everyone into a brooding silence.

Detective-Superintendent Heyhoe walked straight into this silence and stood in the centre of the room radiating deep suspicion of each and every one of us.

CHAPTER 12

It was too quiet. Outside, we could hear slow footsteps coming down the outer hallway, moving with the measured tread of men matching steps to carry something heavy. Even without Hugh's information, we would have known what they were doing. A ripple of distress passed through the room. Gwenda choked back a sob.

"Hrrmmph . . ." Detective-Superintendent Heyhoe cleared his throat too briskly and too loudly. He didn't succeed in kidding anybody, but I appreciated the attempt. "It's going to be necessary to have a little chat with each of you. Do you think we could use this room?"

"Go right ahead, Superintendent," Evangeline said. She settled herself into a corner of the sofa and smiled at him regally.

"I meant, in privacy, madam. One at a time."

"Our lawyer isn't here yet," Martha pointed out quickly.

"I think he's upstairs with Jasper," Hugh said. "Shall I go and get him?"

"If you would," Martha said. "Please."

"Perhaps you wouldn't mind if I asked a few preliminary questions of someone other than your mother while we're waiting?"

"She's not my mother," Martha said.

"Sorry. I meant, your grandmother," he corrected.

"Martha is *my* daughter," I said hastily, before Martha and Evangeline could both fly into a fury. "And I don't mind answering any of your questions."

Actually, I minded very much. I could think of several dozen questions I would rather not be asked. Especially without a lawyer present. Why did I have to open my big mouth?

"Yes," Detective-Superintendent Heyhoe said unenthusiastically. "We'll come to you later, thank you."

Paradoxically, I was furious. I flounced over and perched on the arm of Martha's chair while Heyhoe turned to the kids.

"Do I understand that all of you share the flat at the top?"

"Maisonette, actually," Ursula said.

"And you're all here now?" The question was pointed. I could not be the only one to remember that he had just been talking to Jasper.

"There's also Anni," Des said reluctantly. "But she didn't come home last night."

"That we know of," Ursula added quietly.

"And you were all living together upstairs?" Heyhoe made it sound like a twenty-four-hour-a-day orgy.

Out of the corner of my eye, I noticed that the Sergeant had quietly moved into a chair and was busy with pen and notebook. What a pity his shorthand couldn't possibly encompass the verbal nuances of his superior.

"Just for the record," Heyhoe said with elaborate casualness, "perhaps you wouldn't mind running over your movements last night. Say, perhaps, from about six p.m. to midnight." He was speaking ostensibly to the kids, but his gaze slid towards Evangeline. I began to feel that I had even more reason to worry than I had feared. What was he getting at?

"That's easy," Gwenda said. "We were all at the cinema— the Silver Scween in the Sky—for the pwemiere of *The Wevenge of the White Squaw*, stawwing Evangeline Sinclair. And she was fabulous in it! That was followed by the weception. It was a totally fantastic evening. A weal twiumph for the gweat Evangeline Sinclair!"

"It *was* quite a pleasant occasion." Evangeline barely refrained from smirking.

"So you were all at the cinema from six p.m. to midnight?"

"Er, actually," Ursula said uneasily. "I wasn't there at all. I—I had a prior engagement."

"Anni was there for the showing," Des said, "but I don't know how long she stayed. I had to leave soon after the film to get to work."

"I left early myself—" I spoke quickly to draw Heyhoe's fire from the kids. "I wasn't feeling terribly well. So I came back here, took a couple of sleeping pills and went to bed. Well before midnight."

"I was there the whole time," Gwenda said. "I'm one of the ushewettes at the Silver Scween in the Sky."

"Thank you," Heyhoe said. The Sergeant's pen was flying over the notebook pages. "That's most helpful. Now, perhaps you could be even more helpful while we try to narrow down our timings."

Martha had remained silent. I carefully avoided looking at her, lest my thoughts became apparent. She had not been able to get a seat for the screening, and both she and Hugh had disappeared from the reception before I left.

Also, I had not seen Anni there at all. That didn't necessarily mean that Des had lied, of course.

"This is just a preliminary inquiry," Heyhoe said encouragingly. "I'll be talking with each of you separately later."

That took care of the encouragement. I didn't trust that sneaky smile of his for one instant. Neither did anyone else. The kids looked at each other and moved closer together.

"Now then . . ." The false heartiness of his voice was not reassuring either. "Perhaps you could give us details—" he turned to Ursula— "of that prior engagement. Where you went, the names of the people you met, how long you were there—"

"No," Ursula said firmly. "I'm afraid I couldn't. It was extremely personal. Private, in fact."

"I see." Heyhoe's face darkened, but he was obviously trying to project an understanding persona. He glanced around at the rest of us and bared a few more teeth. "Well, we'll come back to that question when we're alone.

"Meanwhile—" he fixed Des with a relentless gaze— "perhaps you wouldn't mind telling us where you were working last night and what time your gig broke up."

"Actually—" Des swallowed, but could not be less brave than Ursula—"I would. It was a private party. I couldn't say anything more about it without the express permission of my employers."

"I see." Heyhoe nodded as though he had expected nothing better. "We'll take that up in private, too. Meanwhile, perhaps you'd get on to the telephone and get that permission from your employers."

"It will take a while," De said. "It was a farewell party. They've flown back to Saudi Arabia. I don't have a telephone number for them—and I don't know when they'll be back in England again."

Heyhoe turned an interesting shade of purple. I couldn't blame him. It was a good story, but Des was not a good liar. He spoke too loudly, he met no eye, and a nervous tic had begun twitching at the side of his mouth. He might even be speaking the truth, but the way he spoke it he would never get the benefit of any doubt.

"And you—" Heyhoe glared at Gwenda. "You say you were at the cinema—?"

"Evewy minute," Gwenda assured him. "We worked flat out all evening, fwom showing people to their seats for the pwemiere to handing wound canapés and dwinks at the weception. And then Evangeline was kind enough to give me a lift home in her taxi. We got back to the house about one a.m. and I went stwaight to bed. I was exhausted."

"Hmmm . . ." Heyhoe casually slipped a question in Evangeline's direction. "And I suppose you went to bed exhausted, too, madam?"

"On the contrary," Evangeline said. "I was far too exhilarated. It had been a most stimulating occasion. I fixed myself a nightcap and sat up and read for a while. I might add that I heard several people come in and go upstairs."

"I don't suppose you could identify any of them?"

"Certainly not! I was in my room. I didn't get up and go out into the hall to check on them. I'm not a night watchman."

"And you had no curiosity at all about who might be coming in so late?"

"Why should I? It isn't my house."

"You couldn't say which footsteps were male and which were female?"

"Even if I were paying that much attention—which I wasn't—I don't believe I could differentiate."

"You didn't hear any footsteps go out the back way—into the garden?"

"I wouldn't have noticed." Evangeline shrugged. "I had other things to think about."

"Ah yes, the premiere." Heyhoe spoke with obscure satisfaction, as though they had arrived at their destination after following a long and circuitous route. "Quite a momentous occasion, I understand. One of your early pictures restored and just like new. It must have brought back a lot of memories. The film's outstanding feature, I understand—" he glanced at his cohort and got a faint nod of the head in reply—"was the melodramatic ending portraying a certain . . . disposition of the corpses—"

"See here, Hee-Haw—" Evangeline's eyes flashed dangerously. "Are you trying to insinuate that I was so overcome by nostalgia that I went out and scalped that poor boy just for Old Time's Sake?"

"Don't let him trick you!" Martha cried. "Don't say another word until the lawyer gets here!"

"I can do without the vote of confidence, thank you, Martha."

"Shh, please, Martha," I whispered. "You're just making matters worse." Now Heyhoe knew that Martha didn't trust Evangeline's mental stability.

"But you heard him," Martha wailed. "How much worse can they get?"

We found out.

"This is your daughter, madam?" Heyhoe zeroed in on me. "A bit highly-strung, isn't she?"

"She's just not the trusting type," I said. "And she's had a terrible day—she discovered the body."

"Ah yes," Heyhoe said. "I was going to ask about that. Went walking in the garden, didn't she? Strange thing to do in weather like this." He waited expectantly.

The silence told him that he had struck a nerve. The trouble was, he didn't know which nerve.

"She just wanted a breath of air," I said quickly. At any minute, he might decide it was time to start questioning us all separately. It was essential to establish a general line we could all stick to. As Evangeline had pointed out earlier, we didn't want publicity given to the erroneous idea that I might have taken an overdose of sleeping pills.

"Ah yes, madam." Now I had drawn Heyhoe's fire. "You

were at the premiere, too, weren't you? That means everyone here has seen—or heard about—that film and the famous scalping scene."

"Oh, don't!" Gwenda cracked abruptly. "It's *Mick* who died like that. Mick! How can you talk about it like that? It's—it's *wotten* of you!" She burst into sobs.

"What's going on here?" Hugh returned with a stranger at his heels, presumably the lawyer. "Are you harassing these youngsters?"

"Here, now, honey—" Beauregard Sylvester was right behind them. He crossed to Gwenda and put an arm around her shoulders. "Don't take on so. It's going to be all right."

"All wight?" Gwenda shook herself free. "How can it be? Mick's dead—*dead*! Nothing will ever be all wight again!"

"Dear Beau," Evangeline sighed. "He always means so well—and he always says the wrong thing. There's only one way to handle this." She went over to Gwenda and dealt her a brisk slap.

"Take a deep breath—" She caught her by the shoulders and shook her lightly. "Straighten up. That's it. Keep on deep-breathing. Someone get her a glass of water—"

Martha leapt from her chair in response to the command and nearly collided with Jasper in the doorway. Jasper was looking pale and shaken. He made directly for the abandoned chair and sank down into it.

I looked at him thoughtfully, then got off my perch on the arm of the chair and tried not to be too ostentatious about putting some distance between us. I had not forgotten that it was probably the death of his unmourned girlfriend that was responsible for this train of events. Most probably. Only Mick could have told for certain—and Mick was going to tell no tales. Someone had seen to that.

Meanwhile, the police were working blind, without half the vital information they ought to have. Evangeline would have a fit if I tried to supply it. I wasn't too keen on the idea myself. It would lead to an awful lot more questions, like why had we concealed the death in the first place? I wasn't even sure of the answer myself any more.

Perhaps I could send the police an anonymous letter . . . very anonymous. There must be no possible way they could connect it with either me or Evangeline. It would have to be very carefully worded . . .

Beau had drifted over to Ursula and was patting her shoulder. She seemed to be appreciating his particular brand of sweetness and light more than Gwenda had. Des was gently stroking his clarinet, looking off into the distance and shuddering occasionally.

Heyhoe had momentarily retreated from the whole scene under guise of conferring with his sergeant, but those beady little eyes weren't missing a trick. He had seen me move away from Jasper, he noted that Evangeline was getting Gwenda back under control, and the eyes narrowed as Martha returned, carrying a glass of water.

His suspicions were infectious. For a split second, I looked at Martha through his eyes: past her first youth, thin-skinned and highly-strung—as neurotic, in fact, as it was possible to be and still remain uncertified. *Had* she strolled to the end of the garden and, finding Mick there, possibly dozing on the garden bench, impulsively scalped him?

Except—common sense reasserted itself—why should she be carrying a sharp knife on a stroll through the garden? And why on earth would Mick be asleep on the bench in a thick wet fog? No, someone had found Mick there—but it hadn't been Martha. Nor was it likely that Mick had been asleep. He had more probably already been dead. The inevitable autopsy would produce the reason.

It would also tell us whether he had still been alive when he had been scalped. I hoped not. Surely he couldn't have been. There would have been signs of a fearful struggle. He must have been dead—or dying and deeply unconscious—before such an atrocity could have been perpetrated.

Unconscious . . . or dying . . . or dead. Someone had entered my room after I had fallen asleep last night and taken away all my sleeping pills. Almost a full bottle—a fatal dose. Had they been dissolved in a drink of some sort and given to the unsuspecting Mick?

Abruptly, I needed to sit down. I tried to collapse gracefully into the corner seat of the sofa. Unfortunately, this meant I was now facing Jasper. I looked away.

This was a mistake. It put me in eye-to-eye contact with

Heyhoe and he came over to me. I tried not to quail as he loomed above me, but had to remind myself that they didn't have the Third Degree in this country, that we were slightly too important for him to risk using it if they had—and besides there were too many witnesses.

Not that anyone seemed to be paying any attention. Even Martha had her back turned towards me as she urged more water on Gwenda.

"You and Miss Sinclair have known each other a long time, haven't you?" Heyhoe asked.

"Practically for ever." That chummy air didn't fool me; he'd been talking to his film buff sergeant too long and too earnestly. I made a mental bet that I was about to be served up with another rehashed version of The Feud.

"Good friends all your lives, eh?"

"I wouldn't say that. Most friendships have their ups and downs—especially in Hollywood."

"Really?" He looked disappointed. Obviously, he'd hoped to catch me in some sort of lie about "never a cross word."

"There were *years* when we didn't speak to each other," I admitted honestly. "But, after just so long, it gets to seem silly and so, when we ran into each other at a party, we got talking again and made a date for lunch the next day and diplomatic relations were restored."

"And the friendship was restored, too?"

"Wasn't that what I just said?" I noticed that the sergeant had sneaked up behind us, notebook at the ready. "Anyway, it was what I meant."

"And no lingering hard feelings? No regrets? No grudge still being nursed?"

"None," I said firmly. "I've even forgotten what it was all about in the first place." That had been my story for years and this was no time to start changing it. I didn't like the way these questions were going.

"And does Miss Sinclair remember?"

"I wouldn't know. We've never discussed it." I tried to be unobtrusive about signalling over his shoulder for help. This was getting serious.

"How did you like the film last night?" He changed tack, alarming me even more. "Had you seen it before?"

"I saw it the first time round. I was just a child, of course. I saw it at a Saturday matinee."

"Children were allowed to see a film with all that horror and violence?" Heyhoe's voice expressed open disbelief. "Over here, it would have had an X Certificate."

"Violence never bothered anybody when I was a kid. All they ever censored was sex. Today they don't seem to bother about that, either."

"Seeing that film at an impressionable age—didn't it haunt you? Give you nightmares?"

"American kids are tougher than that." I tried a careless laugh. "It was just one of a bunch of scary movies. We had ways of dealing with them. When the action got too tense, somebody would throw a popcorn box at the screen. They did it for love scenes, too. Then boxes would fly at the screen from all directions. Empty boxes, of course, we rarely got so carried away that we wasted good popcorn. Everybody whooped and hollered and, by the time the ushers got us quieted down, the worst of the action was over and we settled back until things got too exciting again."

Heyhoe winced. He did not seem to find my reminiscences of childhood filmgoing as lovable as I fondly remembered them. His sergeant, on the other hand, was busily scribbling in his notebook.

"So . . ." Heyhoe said consideringly, "you were hardened to scenes of violence at an early age."

"Now wait a minute," I protested. "I didn't say that. Just what are you driving at?" As if I didn't know. As if I couldn't see that he was considering the possibility that I had killed Mick, for whatever reason of my own, and then scalped him to throw the blame on Evangeline, thus getting revenge for whatever she had done to me in the past.

"Oh, nothing, nothing. Much too early to be driving at anything at this stage of inquiries. I'm only exploring possible avenues . . ."

"Well, you can forget that one—it's a dead end." Too late, I realized my choice of expression might not have been the wisest. With relief, I saw that Des had caught my mute appeal and had drifted over to us.

I appreciated the gallant gesture and was sorry that it attracted unwelcome notice to him.

"Ah—" Heyhoe looked at him coldly. "Remembered where they had the party last night, have you?"

"Somebody else was driving." Des promptly produced more explanations. "I wasn't paying any attention. I don't know where we went. I just know it was a big house with lots of people."

"Ah yes, all those jet-setting Arabs. Undoubtedly, some-one there will remember you—if we ever find any of them. Meanwhile, perhaps you'd be good enough to give me the name of that driver."

"Er, Dave, I think. Yes, I'm pretty sure. Dave."

"I don't suppose he has a surname?"

"I don't know it. It was all pretty informal. They're not my usual group. I met them in a pub and they needed one more for the gig. They invited me to sit in."

"Ah yes, the proverbial meeting in the pub and the impromptu arrangements." Heyhoe spoke wearily, he had heard it all before. He didn't believe it then and he didn't believe it now.

To be honest, neither did I. I began to wonder just what Des had really been doing last night that he was so anxious to conceal.

CHAPTER 13

"I don't trust them," Martha said. "I don't trust a single one of them. Let's get out of this awful house. Let's move to a hotel. Right now!"

"I'm glad you managed to restrain those sentiments until Hi-Ho left. You might as well keep calm and make the best of it. I'm sure the police wouldn't allow us to leave now."

"They might be able to keep us in the country," Martha argued, "but they can't force us to remain in this house. I'll start packing."

"I don't want to move anywhere," I said. "On the contrary, I just want to lie down." I also wanted to get rid of Martha. I had a few things to discuss with Evangeline, any one of which was guaranteed to send Martha into hysterics.

"So do I," Evangeline quavered and suddenly looked very frail. "This has all been most exhausting and a great shock. I do believe I have one of my frightful headaches coming on."

"Neither of you will need to do a thing," Martha began organizing. "I'll call some hotels and get us a reservation, then I'll do all the packing."

"Oh no you won't!" Evangeline rallied amazingly. "I mean, I do think we should stay here. What's the point of leaving? The damage has been done. Nothing worse can happen."

"What makes you think so?" Martha challenged. "That boy is dead. Somebody killed him and then—then *scalped* him. And you know perfectly well that policeman thinks it was you!"

"All the more reason for not running away. It would be taken as an admission of guilt." Evangeline lifted her head, straightened her back and stared soulfully upwards—the same pose she had used as *Joan of Arc* when the soldiers

105

began to light the brushwood at her feet. "I must stay and prove my innocence."

"And how do you propose to do that?" Martha and I were rarely on the same side, but sheer irritation at Evangeline occasionally united us. If Evangeline had developed hare-brained notions of running around sleuthing, perhaps moving to some hotel as far away from the scene of the crime as possible was not a bad idea.

"Just remember—" Evangeline smiled smugly—"I always solved the crimes in *The Happy Couple* series."

"Just remember you had a script."

"I shall watch for signs of guilt. I shall observe everyone closely—"

There was no use talking to her, she was lost in her fantasy.

"Don't be silly," Martha snapped. "You're far too old!"

"Age does not wither the powers of observation."

I observed that, if there had been a tomahawk handy, Martha's scalp would have been parted from her skull in two seconds flat. Why, after all my efforts, had Martha never learned a bit of tact?

"You go and rest, Mother—" The combination of an order and unwanted concern promptly alienated me again. "I'll start telephoning."

"I'm not moving to any hotel," Evangeline said. "But you can, if you want to," she added hopefully.

"Yes," I chimed in, without any real hope. "You go ahead, but I think I ought to stay here with Evangeline."

"I'm not going without you." Martha reacted as I had feared. "We all go together—or none of us will go!"

"Frankly, dear," Evangeline sighed. "I preferred the version of *The Three Musketeers* with Doug Fairbanks in it."

"Why don't you both go and lie down and try to get some sleep? Have a little nap." Martha switched to sweet reasonableness. "After some rest, perhaps you'll come to your senses. Meanwhile, I'll check out some hotels." She exited, still smiling sweetly.

"Martha—" Evangeline brooded—"is the sort of woman poor, dear John Barrymore was talking about when he said,

'There's only one way to fight a woman—with your hat. Grab it and run!'"

"At least, we're alone now and can talk. Look, we've got to tell Heyhoe about that dead girlfriend of Jasper's. He's working in the dark if he doesn't know that. And we ought to tell him about all my missing sleeping pills, too."

"Stuff and nonsense!" Evangeline snorted, reverting to her Ethel Barrymore best, presumably since she had just been thinking about dear John. "We'll do nothing of the sort. He's the detective. Let him find out for himself—if he can."

"How can he when he doesn't even know where he should be looking? We're distorting the whole case by not giving him the information he needs."

"Hmmph!" This thought was not going to disturb Evangeline unduly. Those had been the conditions that prevailed in every thriller she had ever made. But Heyhoe was a far cry from Jimmie Gleason and Bill Demarest.

"Look—" I tried again despairingly. "These aren't comedy cops. We're up against the real thing—and we could be in real trouble."

"Oh, you always exaggerate so, Trixie. They can't do anything to us—we're stars!"

"We *were* stars." Now I was getting worried. Her grip on reality was slipping again. "That was a long time ago. We don't have the Studios behind us any more. In fact, the Studios aren't there any more. We're on our own, six thousand miles from home—this is no time to play games."

"Oh, Trixie, sometimes you get as boring as Martha! We are not without influence in this country, remember. Dear Beau is a person of some consequence here and we can rely on his protection."

"Oh yeah? If Heyhoe pins this rap on either of us, I'll give you odds that your precious Beau will disappear so fast you won't see him for dust." I'd been in a few thrillers myself.

"So—" Evangeline's eyes narrowed as she fell into the familiar script—"you think we ought to rat on the boys?"

"I think we ought to sing like canaries." I found I had not lost the knack (acquired for *Gold Diggers Behind Bars*) of talking without moving my lips. "Mick's dead, nothing we can say can harm him now."

"What about the others?" Evangeline dropped the act abruptly. "Mick was trying to protect them."

"One of them doesn't deserve protection," I reminded her darkly. "The others will have to take their chances." A momentary cynicism overcame me. "Who knows how deep they're all in it, anyway?"

"I wonder—" Evangeline mused. "I just wonder where that boy, Des, got to last night? He's acting as though he's hiding the Guilty Secret of all time."

"And, these days, guilt isn't what it used to be." I didn't want to suspect Des, but Evangeline had a point there. "Nowadays, people cheerfully admit to things they'd have paid blackmail to keep quiet in our time."

"Flaunting it," Evangeline said bitterly. "When I think what you and I went through just to—"

"Maybe we'd better forget about that. There are too many people getting interested. Even Heyhoe was asking questions. He seems to think we might have buried the hatchet, but not the feud. He's pussy-footing towards the theory that I dug up the hatchet and used it on Mick to try to make it look as though you did it."

"That's an improvement over his theory that I was overcome by nostalgia and decided to treat myself to one last scalp on my belt."

"It's only an improvement so far as you're concerned. I'm not overjoyed about it myself."

Evangeline didn't quite turn her snicker into a cough in time.

"I'm glad you think it's funny." My own sense of humour had been in abeyance since I awoke this morning to find our little chums working me over. "Perhaps they'll hang me— and then you can have a real laugh!"

"Don't be absurd, they abolished the death penalty here years ago."

"They're bringing it back in the States. Who knows what will happen next? You may get lucky—"

A knock at the door brought us both to attention. We broke off our squabble and looked at each other.

"I'll go," I said.

"We'll both go." Evangeline closed ranks. We marched together to the door and opened it.

"Er, hello—" Des stood there, fidgeting nervously under our challenging stares. "I—Uh, *we* . . . Uh, it's long past lunchtime and none of us has had anything to eat. I'm going down to the Chinese takeaway—" He waved a menu at us. "What do you fancy?"

"Everything!" Suddenly, I realized I was starving. No wonder I had been self-pitying and snappish. I couldn't even remember when I had last sent anything reasonably solid down to my long-suffering stomach.

"Beef-and-green-peppers, fried rice, chicken subgum and noodles." Evangeline ordered rapidly, not even glancing at the menu.

"Peking duck," I decided, "perhaps some plain boiled rice, king prawns, and Martha likes sweet-and-sour-pork—"

"Wait a minute," Evangeline said. "I'll get my purse."

"No, please," Des said. "You're our guests—all of you." He took a deep breath. "If you don't mind eating with us. Gwenda and Ursula are brewing up tea and we'll mix everything together. That's what Chinese meals are all about, isn't it?"

"That sounds marvellous," I said warmly. "But you really must let us pay for our own—"

"No, honestly, we have plenty of money. You're our guests, please. It will be our pleasure . . ." He moved off to the sound of coins jingling in every pocket.

"Those poor, sweet lambs," I said, "they must have emptied their piggy banks. But I suppose we must allow them their pride."

"We'll make it up to them later," Evangeline said. "Next time, we can claim it's our turn and take them out someplace really nice."

"We'll do that before we leave—if they let us leave." Then I remembered something else. "I wonder what's happened to Anni?"

Martha grumbled, but followed us upstairs. She objected to dining with a group of suspects in a lurid murder, but the only alternative was to go out and find a restaurant on her own; then there would be the inevitable long wait for her order to arrive. She hadn't eaten in a long while, either, so hunger won out over prejudice.

I was not surprised to find that Beau had left—Chinese takeaways weren't exactly his style. Hugh was talking earnestly to Jasper in a corner; they rose to their feet as we entered.

"Weally!" Gwenda bustled about, settling Evangeline and myself into the best armchairs. Martha, she left to her own devices. "The questions those policemen asked! It was disgwaceful! They see a mixed gwoup of young people in a flat—and they jump to one conclusion. They have absolutely filthy minds!"

"*And* you're theatrical people," Evangeline commiserated. " 'Twas ever thus. We're always suspect, you know. Thieves, vagabonds and rogues—the old feelings about us have never quite disappeared."

"That's wight!" Gwenda brightened. Evangeline's liberal use of the plural had cheered her immoderately. "*We* do meet with a lot of jealousy and suspicion fwom non-theatwicals." She preened slightly. "People can be so silly. Do let me get you another cushion—"

"I'm quite comfortable, thank you."

But Gwenda had darted off in search of a cushion. Hugh, I noticed with interest, had abandoned Jasper and was now deep in conversation with Martha. She seemed to be complaining—probably about us—nothing new about that. Hugh was nodding his head and making soothing noises.

Jasper had wandered over to the window and was looking down on the carriageway. I approached him casually and also looked down at the carriageway.

"Have the police all gone?" The carriageway was deserted, but someone might still be on guard in the garden.

"For the time being," he said gloomily. "They'll be back when they think of some more questions. Probably after the . . . the autopsy."

"It *is* a disturbing thought." I tried to sound sympathetic. This was the second of Jasper's friends to be autopsied. I wondered if he knew that. I also wondered how I could find out. I wasn't supposed to know anything about it. I couldn't just ask him if he'd noticed he was one girlfriend short lately.

"Has Anni come back yet?" Perhaps I could lead him towards a gradual realization that more than one girl was missing.

"Anni?" He looked vaguely startled and turned away from the window, scanning the room. "I haven't seen her . . ."

"Strange that she should disappear last night, of all nights," I mused. "You don't suppose she had anything to do with it, do you?"

"No, she couldn't. Not Anni." He shook his head dazedly. "I'll grant you it's strange that she . . . disappeared, but no stranger than what happened to Mick." He shook his head again. "It's all a nightmare."

"Maybe she saw something. Maybe the killer took her away."

"You mean, she's dead, too?" I had him on the ropes. I only wished I knew what that *too* meant. How many bodies was he counting?

"I'm not sure what I mean," I said honestly. "I only know the whole situation makes me very uneasy. And poor Martha is a nervous wreck."

"I can see that." He looked across the room at Martha, who was acting more distraught by the minute. Hugh wasn't being the calming influence I had hoped.

"It must have been quite terrible for her . . . finding him like that." There was something wrong about his tone. I looked up at him in surprise—and caught the expression on his face.

He suspected Martha! It was written in every lineament. He actually thought Martha had—for neurotic reasons best known to herself—killed Mick and then scalped him, and then pretended to discover his body. Or maybe he thought, having done the foul deed, she had given way to an attack of hysteria and pretended that it was because she had stumbled over the body.

"Oh!" My gasp was inaudible. I was so startled I could not speak. If he could think that, then it must mean that he hadn't done it himself. He was innocent.

Either that, or he was the best actor of the lot and was wasted in the stockbrokerage. That, too, was possible.

"Here we are—" Ursula bustled into the room juggling

an assortment of flat-surfaced items. "I thought it would be more convenient if we ate off trays. We don't have enough room in the kitchen."

So that's what they were supposed to be. She dealt out the makeshift trays. I got one which looked as though it had just been snatched off a dressing-table and hastily dusted off hairpins and powder. Martha got a baking tray and Evangeline, being guest of honour, got the only *bona fide* tray in the lot. It got worse as she reached those she obviously considered family. Jasper got an oven pan and Gwenda a cake plate.

There was a thump at the door and Gwenda flew to open it. Des stood there, laden down with bulging Chinese takeaway carrier bags. Delicious fragrances wafted from the bags as he went through the living-room to the kitchen; he no longer jingled when he walked. I realized just how hungry I was.

So was everyone else. They wasted no time dishing out the food into an assortment of crockery even more eccentric than the trays and we got down to the serious business of eating. I noted that the flatmates were eating directly from the takeaway cartons and wondered if it would hurt their pride if we gave them a matched set of dinnerware as a parting gift.

"Isn't this fun, Twixie?" Gwenda brought her carton over and sat on the floor at my feet. "At least," her face clouded, "it would be if it weren't for the circumstances. Oh, Twixie—"

"Never mind that right now," I said hastily. "You just get some food into you. You'll feel better then."

"I'll twy . . ." She sighed and rapidly began to demolish the savoury contents of her carton. She looked better after the first few mouthfuls.

Ursula, having bagged the seat next to Evangeline, spent a great deal of time hopping up and refilling teacups and mugs. Otherwise, we ate rapidly and silently, too hungry to be social.

"My goodness, I needed that," I said happily, as I finished the last bean sprout in my soup bowl. I was even feeling chirpy enough to try an old joke. "I was so hungry my stomach thought my throat was cut."

There was a ripple of nervous laughter, dying away as we slowly realized that it was a rather unfortunate pleasantry, given the circumstances. Of course, it hadn't been a throat that was cut . . . not yet.

"I don't like it," Jasper said abruptly. He did not mean the feeble joke. He had been brooding silently throughout the meal. "Anni should have been back by now—even if she stayed somewhere else last night. Hasn't she telephoned?"

"No, we've had no word at all." Ursula looked frightened. "You don't think—"

"I don't like it," Jasper said again.

"We're not exactly cwazy about it ourselves."

"Doesn't anyone have any idea where she might be?" Evangeline was growing impatient with the casual attitude of the flatmates. "Why don't you start telephoning her friends and ask if they've seen her?"

"We could," Ursula said, "if we knew who they were. We only share a flat, you know, not an address book. We each have our own circle of friends and we've only ever met a few of each other's friends—and then it was at casual parties and we wouldn't have bothered with last names."

"How awkward." Evangeline gave an exaggerated sigh, but it had been the same in theatrical hostels in our early days. Only the public imagined that we were one great friendly amorphous mass. We were always aware that we were distinct personalities, with our own cliques, claques, friendships, loves—and hates. And, of course, if anyone had a particularly dishy male on the string, he was kept well away from the competition.

The telephone rang in the hallway.

"Anni!" Gwenda leaped to her feet, radiant with relief. "It must be Anni! I'll get it." She dashed out into the hallway.

We settled back limply, smiling weakly at each other. How silly we had been to worry. Everything was all right. Of course, it was all right.

An agonized howl suddenly reverberated through the room.

"If this continues—" Evangeline raised a nerveless hand to her forehead—"I shall have to buy some ear plugs."

CHAPTER 14

"No-o-o . . ." Gwenda wailed in anguish. "No! No! No!" She slammed down the receiver and burst into tears.

"Gwenda!" "Gwenda!" We made a concerted dash for the hall. "Was it Anni?" "Gwenda, what's the matter?"

"Child, what did they say?" I found Gwenda had hurled herself at me and, head on my shoulder, was sobbing her heart out.

"I can't," she choked. "I won't! They can't make me do it!"

"There, there, of course, they can't." I patted her comfortingly. "Do what?"

"Who was it?" Ursula demanded. "Was it Anni? What's the matter?"

"Oh, it's tewwible, tewwible." Gwenda raised her head and looked at us tragically. "The news is out. It's been on wadio. Television will have it in the next news pwo-gwamme. That was Mummy on the phone. She's insisting that I come home immediately. To stay. To Llandudno—in November!"

"Inhuman!" Ursula breathed.

"Tell her the police won't let you." Des had more practical advice.

"You shouldn't have hung up on her," Hugh fretted. "She'll only ring back. When she does, let me speak to her. Perhaps I can calm her. You really can't leave London now, you know."

That information did a lot towards calming Gwenda, whatever it might do for her mother.

"I'm all wight, weally." She straightened and gave herself a little shake. "It's just that it was so unexpected—"

The telephone rang again. Hugh started forward.

"No—let me." Gwenda picked up the receiver and listened cautiously, then her face cleared. "It's for you—" She held the receiver out to Des.

Never send to know for whom the bell tolls . . . Des paled, but took a deep breath and manfully grasped the receiver.

"Yes?" His shoulders slumped. It was just what he had expected. "Hello, Mum, Dad. Yes, yes, I'm fine. We're all fine—well, almost all."

The receiver crackled briefly. Des opened his mouth and made several croaking sounds, unsuccessfully trying to stem the flow. It was the same all over the world. I had momentarily lost sight of the fact that they were so very young. Of course, they had parents who were still vigorous, commanding—and influential.

"I don't think our MP can do anything about this, Dad—" At last Des got a word in edgewise. "I mean, it's not his sort of territory, is it? Anyway, the police have been quite good, really. No, no, I can't. They won't let us leave. Quite customary. No—" His voice rose in anguish. "No, don't do anything. You'll only make things worse. Yes, yes, I promise I'll get on to you immediately if there's anything you can do—"

After a few more assurances and protestations, Des replaced the receiver, looking as though he had just gone through the proverbial mill. The telephone rang again almost immediately.

Ursula backed away from it, an expression of dread in her eyes. It could only be for her . . . or Anni.

"Tchah!" With an impatient exclamation, Evangeline strode forward and snatched up the receiver. As she did so, her face changed, lengthened, her skin grew tauter, even her eyes seemed to slant slightly.

"Hong Fu Lo Chinese Takeaway," she intoned in a singsong chant. "Today's Special. Foo Young Dan . . ."

The other party slammed down their receiver in exasperation. Evangeline clicked the cradle, then set the receiver down on the table beside the telephone.

"Press," she announced briskly. "They'll keep getting a busy signal from now on, but that won't hold them for long. They'll be on their way now. Let's get out of here."

"Cwumbs!" Gwenda glanced at her watch. "It's time for me to get to the Silver Scween. I'll be late—" She dashed for her room.

"Why don't we all go to Cinema City?" Ursula suggested. "They won't think of looking for us there."

"We've seen the film, thank you," Evangeline said drily.

"Ah, but you haven't seen the whole cinema complex," Ursula said. "The entire floor below the actual cinema holds the archives and the laboratory—that's where I work. Now that we've successfully restored *Revenge of the White Squaw*, and copied it onto acetate safety film, we've begun work on *Scars On Her Soul*. Come and see. I think you'll be pleased with what we're doing."

There was a sudden commotion out in the carriageway below, a roar of several motors, voices shouting . . .

"Oh, God!" Hugh was the first to reach the window. He looked down on the scene with despair. "It's the BBC and ITV OB vans!"

"Oh, do speak English," Evangeline said crossly.

"The Television Outside Broadcast vans," Hugh translated. "Yes, and some radio cars, as well. Plus assorted journalists and photographers—" An engine gunned, brakes shrieked below. "There are more of them arriving every minute. We're besieged!"

"We can go out the back way," Jasper said. "It isn't too bad—" He smiled encouragingly at Evangeline and me. "There's a gate in the fence that leads into the next street. That's a cul-de-sac, so no one will think of our escaping that way. Not until it's too late, I hope. We can cut through and pick up a taxi at St. John's Wood Roundabout. But we'll have to hurry before the Press think of posting a lookout at the back door."

The front doorbell pealed sharply. After the briefest pause, it pealed again, then continued to ring incessantly.

"It's going to be a war of nerves," Evangeline said. She had experienced these sieges before. We both had.

"I'll go and keep them occupied while you get away," Hugh said nobly. "So long as they have someone standing in front of them saying, 'No comment,' it will keep them occupied."

"I'm weady." Gwenda came back into the room. "Are we leaving now?"

"This very minute," Evangeline said firmly. "Martha, fetch our coats and we'll be on our way."

* * *

We leaned over the Moviola watching the miniature figures go through their paces. They seemed distant and remote, more like memories than an actual film. Of course, full-size, projected onto a proper screen, the film would come into its own again.

"I *love* this bit," Ursula said earnestly. She looked at me approvingly. "It's your death scene."

"Thanks," I said ironically, but I could not quite repress a shudder. Someone had just walked over my grave.

"I always loved that part myself," Evangeline said. She had had the picture to herself after I was out of the way, the whole closing reel of it.

But this was the scene the critics had raved over. Stills from it featured in every book of cinema history. I had come close to an Academy Award for this one, my first nomination as Best Supporting Actress.

"Oooh, yes, it's tewwific—" Gwenda had slipped down to join us after the film had started upstairs. "Oh, if I could only learn to act like that, I'd die happy!"

"Shh!" Ursula said sharply. "It's starting now."

We concentrated on the tiny figures reaching out to us from a world—a lifetime—away.

My Chorus-Girl-with-a-Heart-of-Gold and Evangeline, my childhood friend and now a big Broadway star, faced each other across the luxurious Art Deco drawing-room of the gangster's lair. She had taken him away from me. I didn't really want him, but I knew that he was poison for her. He would cost her her reputation, her career, perhaps even her life. We began to quarrel soundlessly—the Moviola was without sound reproduction equipment.

Enter the gangster, the law not far behind on his heels. He rushes to the desk to get hold of and destroy the incriminating evidence before the District Attorney's men arrive. He ignores both of us. We hurl ourselves at him, begging him to pay attention to us, to make a decision. He shakes us off impatiently. There's no time for women now.

There was no time for anything. Beauregard Sylvester, the Assistant District Attorney, burst through the doorway, chest heaving with what looked like emotion if you didn't know that the Director had made him run three times around the set in order to induce a state of breathlessness that would look like emotion.

Evangeline, who had once been engaged to him before she became infatuated with the villain, fell back, hand pressed to heart. I, too, stepped back out of the way to give hero and villain a clear view of each other for the big confrontation.

Beauregard was alone, anxious to save the reputation of his beloved, to get her out of here before the squad cars arrived—and the photographers. He snapped an order at her. She did not move. The villain sent her a craven smile and held out his hand, seeing her now as his only chance to escape.

Frozen with indecision, she could not move. In the distance, sirens were wailing as the police cars drew near. The villain hurriedly stuffed the last of the vital documents into his briefcase and started for the door.

Beau moved to block his way. They stared at each other across the intervening space, then the villain pulled a gun. He had nothing to lose, he would fry anyway if they caught him. His intention was clear to see. His finger tightened on the trigger. Beau was doomed—or was he?

Evangeline might be paralysed, but I was not. I rushed forward into the path of the speeding bullet. I would save her true love for her (also I was a bit sweet on him myself). The bullet struck me and I collapsed.

The villain dashed away and Beau gave chase. As I lay dying, Evangeline moved at last. She came forward and knelt beside me, cradling me in her arms, recognizing my sacrifice, realizing what a fool she had been.

Evangeline and I glanced at each other with wry smiles above the Moviola and the absorbed heads of our newest audience. In my mind, I could hear the violins that had played throughout the scene.

"I've seen this bit eight times already," Ursula said, with a catch in her voice. "And it still makes me cry."

On the tiny screen, Evangeline and I stared silently into each other's eyes. Her hand supported my head, I clung to her other hand with both of mine. Slowly her eyes filled with tears. We were saying the long goodbye.

"It's tewwific," Gwenda breathed. "simply tewwific. The

way you look at each other. All that love, all that understanding . . ." She sniffled and groped for her handkerchief. "It's heart-bweaking. . . ."

Yes, the critics had reacted that way, too. They had
written lyrically of "the silent struggle to express themselves in these final moments."

No one knew what a genuine struggle it had been.
Evangeline had been doing her best—or worst—to steal
the closeup. Throughout that affecting scene, she had been
wrestling with my head, trying to turn my face against her
bosom so that the back of my head would be to the camera.

Naturally, I wasn't going to take that lying down. Out of
camera range, I caught her little finger and slowly bent it
backwards. That was when those big expressive eyes
gradually filled with tears. Our silent battle raged while the
cameras turned. Then, just short of a broken or dislocated
finger, she gave up and stopped trying to turn my face away
from the camera.

After that, I released her finger and died like a lady.

On the miniature screen, the tension snapped. The
Chorus-Girl-with-a-Heart-of-Gold gave one last chipper
little smile and sagged in Evangeline's arms. The camera
dwelt lovingly on my closed eyes, then panned up to
Evangeline's face as a tear slid down her cheek and her lips
quivered.

Happily, the boom mike failed to pick up the word she
murmured at me. Fade-out.

"Oh, that was so beautiful," Gwenda sobbed.

"I told you I always cried," Ursula sniffled.

Hugh, who had slipped in quietly while the scene was
running, was blinking rapidly. I turned to take the handkerchief count of the rest of our audience. Des and Jasper
seemed quite impressed, too.

"I suppose it's really quite a nice little period piece."
Trust Martha! She was unmoved. Of course she had seen it
before, but so had Ursula—and Ursula always cried.

"Oh, what a pity!" Martha leaned forward and frowned at
the Moviola critically. "The rest of the print is ruined. What
a shame."

The next scene, a long shot of Beau chasing the villain,
was running through the machine and we all stared glumly

at the starbursts, scratches and pinpoints of light character-
istic of a deteriorating film.

"No—it's not hopeless." Ursula snapped off the machine.
The tiny screen went dark. "We just haven't got round to
restoring that bit yet. We worked on the major scenes first."

"Oh?" Martha was nonplussed. "I thought you'd start at
the beginning and work your way through chronologically."

"Sometimes we do, but when the film is in a bad state,
the priority is to save the key scenes. We can patch up the
linking scenes later. We don't particularly like doing it that
way, but sometimes it's necessary."

"Apart from which," Hugh said, "it's dangerous to have
too much of that old nitrate film lying around. The stuff is
too volatile—flammable. Beau stores the film not actually
being worked on in an outbuilding at his country place.
And these rooms are all fireproofed, you may have noticed.
Even so, the insurance situation might be tricky if anything
should happen."

I had noticed, as we entered, the reinforced steel door,
like that of a bank vault. Presumably the floors and ceiling
were similarly reinforced. It could be very nasty if a fire
broke out here, with a crowded cinema directly above. *The
Towering Inferno* wouldn't be in it. For the first time, I
noticed the fire extinguishers clamped to the walls and the
little boxes containing the fireproof blankets used to
smother flames.

"It's really quite safe." Hugh correctly interpreted my
thoughtful stare. "Ideally, of course, the laboratory and
work rooms should be out in the country, too. Beau wanted
it that way, but Juanita refused to countenance it. It was all
he could do to persuade her to allow the old films to be
stored on their property. Unfortunately, she seems to have
taken against films these days—especially the ones in which
she didn't appear herself."

"I'm not surprised," Evangeline said. "Beau and I were a
romantic team long before Juanita appeared on the scene.
It always rankled with her."

"It's iniquitous!" Ursula clenched her fists, the fire and
passion of the true archivist coming to the fore. "Archivists
all over the world are in a race against time to save these
cinematic masterpieces. We need all the help we can get.

And to think that someone who was actually in the Industry can refuse to—"

"I'm afraid the old girl is actually rather a hindrance," Hugh said apologetically. "We've all taken a turn talking to her, but she just won't see reason."

"She was always a jealous cat," Evangeline said. "I'll bet she cooperated all right when it came to her own films."

"Oh yes." A wan smile, reminiscent of battles lost and won flickered on Ursula's lips. "She practically stood over me, trying to tell me how to do it. She seemed to think I could work miracles. I finally had to tell her that my work stopped with the print itself—I couldn't improve her performance."

"Whe-ew!" Jasper whistled. "So that was why she was in such a filthy mood last winter."

"I shouldn't have said it." Ursula was only partially repentent. "But I lost my temper. After that, she went back to the country and locked herself away again. She tried to make Beau stop the whole restoration project. Thank heavens he didn't listen to her."

"Why such urgency?" Martha was puzzled. "What did you mean when you said, you're in a race against time?"

"Because the original film stock was nitrate film and the nitric acid in the stock causes chemical decomposition with the passage of time. It's highly unstable in itself, as well as flammable. Unfortunately, almost all early 35mm films were shot on nitrate stock. The forecast is that most of the early films will have disintegrated beyond restoration by the year 2000. National archives and private archivists all over the world are fighting that deadline to save, restore and copy onto acetate stock as much film as we can."

"I had no idea it was so complicated," Martha said.

"Most people haven't. Even we are still discovering all the complications." Ursula grinned wryly. "Once the films are on acetate, the forecast is that they'll be preserved for another one hundred years, or possibly, two. Provided, of course, that they're stored in optimum conditions. Archivists in tropical climates have already had a nasty shock; they've discovered even the triacetate stock is beginning to decompose in their hot and humid conditions. Experiments are going on now with polyester-based stock.

"So, you see, it's still a race against time. Perhaps the best we can hope for is to gain another century, so that future archivists can save our fragile heritage of film art permanently by recopying the work onto material that hasn't even been invented yet."

Ursula was so intense—and so young. The way she tossed remarks about centuries around. It was beginning to give me a nasty suspicion about her definitions.

"Just how early," I inquired cautiously, "are those early films? When did they stop using nitrate stock?"

"They were using it up until 1951."

"That recently?" Evangeline was as aghast as I. It seemed like only yesterday.

"And I suppose different copies of the film deteriorate at a different rate," Martha said thoughtfully. "Evangeline's copy, for instance, is in a lot better state of preservation than the one you seem to be working from."

"The California climate is probably better for it," Evangeline said. "I should imagine the humidity in England—"

She broke off, becoming aware that everyone in the room was staring at her.

"You—" Ursula took a half-step forward. "You have a copy of *Scars On Her Soul?* A complete copy?"

"Well, it wouldn't be much good if it were partial, would it? Of course I have. I have copies of most of my films. A few companies were too cheap to give me one, but most—"

"Most!" Ursula whispered. "Do you . . . do you have *When Angels Fall?*"

"No," Evangeline said grimly. "I'd fondly imagined we'd destroyed every copy of that."

"But *Flower of the North? Destiny of Darkness?* You have those?"

"Those," Evangeline said complacently, "and *Disposing of Larry, Never Since Eve, The Happy Couple, Beast of the Barbary Coast* . . . Really, dear, it would be simpler for me to tell you the titles I *don't* have."

"Aaah . . . " Ursula's gasp of satisfaction was echoed from the far corner of the room. Jasper met Ursula's eyes and they nodded at each other.

"Beau was right," Jasper said. "She still has the first film she ever made."

And Beau still had the first dollar, but I didn't say it. Evangeline met my eyes and conveyed her own opinion in her Ethel Barrymore voice.

"I believe we have just discovered the real reason why we were so generously invited over here. Retrospective, indeed!"

CHAPTER 15

"I don't know whether I'm feeling my age, or whether some sort of reaction has set in." I kicked off my shoes and collapsed on the sofa, profoundly grateful to be back in our temporary home.

"Probably a bit of both. I'm quite exhausted myself," Evangeline admitted. "Thank heavens Hugh has taken Martha off somewhere."

"Yes . . . Evangeline, do you think there's something brewing there? I mean, do you think it might come to anything? Hugh actually seems to be seeking Martha out. I wouldn't have thought she was his type at all."

"Nonsense, they were made for each other." Evangeline was at the brandy decanter again; we'd have to replenish it in the morning. "He's a masochist, if I ever saw one."

"But Martha's not a sadist," I protested.

"Perhaps not, but she'll keep him apologizing for the rest of his life. He'll have a wonderful time—so will she." Evangeline brought me my glass and raised her own. "Here's to them! You may get that girl off your hands, after all!"

"You're sinking an awful lot of brandy these days." If she could hit below the belt, so could I. "You'd better be careful. That Ethel Barrymore impersonation is all very well—but you don't want people going around saying they could trot a mouse on *your* breath."

"I do *not*—" Evangeline quivered with fury—"impersonate Ethel Barrymore!"

"Since when?"

"Mother! Mother!" Martha began her yodeling out in the front hall and continued all the way into the flat.

"I knew it was too good to be true," Evangeline sighed. "He's dumped her already."

"Mother—" Martha burst into the drawing-room and hurled herself at me. "Mother—" She clung to me.

"What's the matter?" It took a lot to alarm me where Martha was concerned, but I could feel her trembling. "What's happened?"

"Mother—there's someone sleeping in my bed!"

"Oh no!" I cried. "Not again!"

"If you're telling your mother the Story of the Three Bears—" Evangeline covered my slip quickly. "Then you've got that line wrong. It should go, 'Someone's *been* sleeping in my bed'—"

"No," Martha said. "She's still there."

Evangeline and I exchanged uneasy glances. It wasn't possible, of course, but on a night like this, it would be very easy to believe in ghosts.

"What did you mean, Mother?" Martha pushed herself away from me and stared at me. "You said *Not again?*"

"Never mind that now." Evangeline took the words right out of my mouth. "If this isn't your idea of a joke, you'd better show us what you're talking about. Who is it? Do you know?"

"I never saw her before. I—I couldn't look at her too closely—" Martha shuddered. "She looked hideous—grotesque."

"Was she—?" My mouth had gone dry. I swallowed a few times and tried again. "Had she been scalped, too?"

Martha gave a wail of horror and began to cry.

"Oh, come on." Evangeline pushed us aside and started across the hall. "We might as well know the worst."

The form was huddled and still on Martha's bed, but at least she was breathing—in fact, snoring.

"Don't tell me this is Anni?" Even as I spoke, I saw that the hair spread across the pillow was black, so it couldn't be the missing Anni.

"Wake up, you!" With reinforcement behind her, Martha was bolder. She stepped forward and shook the sleeping woman. "Who are you? How did you get in here?"

"Oooh . . ." The figure on the bed moaned, groaned, stretched and rolled over. "Wha—?" Then she sat up, but her face didn't.

"Juanita!" Evangeline was a split second ahead of me in identifying her. "What are *you* doing here?"

"Evangeline—?" Faintly slanted eyes peered up at us from St. Bernard pouches. The tip of her nose seemed twisted and one jowl drooped lower than the other. "How did you get in here?"

"How did you?" Martha snapped. "That's the question. This is *my* room."

"I beg your pardon." Juanita shook herself like a dog coming in out of the rain and her features fell back into place . . . a little. "This is my *pied-à-terre*. It always has been."

"*Dear* Juanita." Evangeline braced herself, then stooped and kissed one lumpy cheek. "You're looking very . . ." Not even she could finish that sentence.

"I know how I look," Juanita said harshly. "I've been trying to spare the world the sight. However, that is no longer possible. I caught the news on television, but they didn't report fully. I had to come to find out for myself. What has been going on here?"

"I wish we knew," Martha said. "We're as much in the dark as anybody else."

Juanita dismissed Martha's plaint with a nod. It did not escape her attention that Evangeline and I had remained silent.

"And what have you two to say for yourselves?" she demanded.

"I might say, 'How do you do,' if anyone bothered to introduce me," I said.

"You must be Trixie Dolan," Juanita said dismissively. "Beau told me you were accompanying Evangeline. But—" she glared at Martha—"who is this?"

"Martha, my daughter. She, er, joined us later."

"Indeed?" Juanita inspected Martha closely, then turned back to us. "I see."

"That's more than I do," Evangeline said. "I understood you chose to remain in the country these days. If you've changed your mind, why come to this house?"

"Where else should I go, when I am needed here?"

"Who needs you?" I realized belatedly that that sounded

ruder than I had intended, but I knew that she would not have rushed to Evangeline's side in any hour of need. They had barely been on speaking terms since the days when Beau was courting Juanita while co-starring with Evangeline.

"I mean," I tried again, "who—?"

"My grandson!" Juanita stood and drew herself up to her full height. The effect was impressive, so long as you didn't look at the face. "He is in trouble. Horrible things have happened under his roof. How could you think I would not come to him—at whatever cost to myself?"

"Jasper!" It had come clear to Evangeline, at least. "I knew there was something familiar about those beady little—I mean, now that I think of it, he *does* remind me of you. And Beau, of course."

"He takes after his father's side of the family," Juanita said contemptuously. "Even to all this stockbroker nonsense."

"It must be a severe trial to you, I'm sure." Evangeline was not as sympathetic as she might be. It was obvious that she felt that the world was not missing out on any great talent if the Sylvester line retreated from the stage.

"I'm tired," Martha complained. (Sometimes, I worried about that girl's stamina.) "This day has gone on forever. I want to go to bed and she's—"

"*She*—" Juanita turned a menacing gaze on her. "*She* is occupying her rightful place in a family home. *You* are trespassing!"

"Oh no I'm not," Martha countered. "I'm paying for this accommodation. I was told it was all right—"

"Obviously," Evangeline said quickly, "since you haven't been coming up to town for such a long while, Jasper thought you wouldn't mind if he let someone else use the place. I take it you've arrived unexpectedly?"

"I telephoned," Juanita said sulkily, "but there was no answer. Naturally, I came straight to my own quarters—I was not to know I had been dispossessed."

"Where am I going to sleep tonight?" Martha's voice began rising. "That's what I want to know."

Never volunteer. That chaise-longue was probably lumpier than Juanita's face. I kept my mouth shut.

"Jasper must be home now," Evangeline said. "Why don't you go up and talk to him, Juanita? If he has the whole flat upstairs, there must be room for you there."

"I have always tried never to invade his privacy," Juanita said. "That is why I have my own quarters. He is young, hot-blooded, he does not want his grandmother playing duenna—"

"Nevertheless—" Evangeline took her arm firmly and steered her towards the door. "I'm afraid he's going to have to put up with it for tonight. Martha is right, it's been a long day and she needs her sleep. We all do. Let's go and throw ourselves on Jasper's mercy."

It was a close thing, but I did not wind up on the chaise-longue in Evangeline's room. I continued to occupy my own room and Martha kept the studio flat across the hall. We found that Jasper, despite his hot blood, was not entertaining female company that night and was gratifyingly glad to see his granny. He happily settled her in his guest room and we all got a good night's sleep.

In the morning, I decided I had had enough—more than enough—of the lot of them. I dressed quickly and quietly, didn't stop for breakfast, just scribbled a note telling them I'd declared a holiday and they could expect me when they saw me, and silently left the house.

Oh, the glorious freedom! I treated myself to Harrod's, a pub lunch, and a matinee of the latest comedy. Then, pausing only for more refreshment, I went on to an evening performance of another show. It left me purring. This was the sort of thing I had come to London to enjoy. Two theatres in one day—this was more like it.

I was so pleased with myself by the end of the evening that I decided to be an absolute daredevil and take the Underground home. After all, millions of people did it every day, it couldn't be all that hard. And I could always ask directions if I got lost—I was in an English-speaking country.

I went into Leicester Square Station and the man didn't seem at all surprised when I asked for a ticket to St. John's Wood, so I figured I was doing all right. An idiot could have read the colour-coded map of the Underground on the wall. Signs were plentiful and those helpful colours kept you heading in the right direction for the line you wanted.

According to the wall map, my best bet was to go to Charing Cross and then change to the Jubilee Line which would take me straight to St. John's Wood Station. It couldn't be simpler.

Except that I must have taken the wrong turning somewhere. I found myself trudging miles of passageways with rounded walls and roof (I could see why it was also called the Tube). I began to think that I was going to walk all the way to St. John's Wood.

I turned yet another corner and went down a deserted passageway. Ahead, I could hear a faint melodic echo which gradually grew louder as I moved nearer, giving the promise of life and human company somewhere deep in these echoing caverns. I hurried my steps, anxious to find the Pied Piper at the end of the corridor.

The music lilted and soared, lifting my heart and tempting my feet to dance. The unknown musician was good—very good. There was something of Benny Goodman about him, not an imitation, just a faint shadowing.

Of course, I turned the final corner and nearly stumbled over him—it was the instrument: the clarinet.

Unexpectedly, the musician blew a sour note and missed the next note altogether. And he had been doing so well.

"Trixie!" It was my fault. He lowered the instrument and stared at me in horror.

"Des!" He had recognized me before I recognized him, but I knew him now. "What are you doing here?"

It would be difficult to say which of us blushed harder then, because it was all too clear what he was doing. Coins gleamed on a square of sacking at his feet. As we stared at each other, mutually aghast, hurrying footsteps sounded behind us and someone pitched a fivepence piece at the sacking. It missed, hit the floor, bounced and rolled.

Automatically, I put my foot on it before it coud get away. Then we both blushed again. This was ridiculous! I stooped, picked up the coin and tossed it on the sacking. "You earned it," I said. "Never be ashamed of money honestly earned. You're a damned good musician. I've worked with a lot and I know. I'm delighted to have had a chance to hear you play."

"Thank you." He seemed overcome. "This is just temporary, you know, until I get a proper job again—"

"Do you think I don't know? Believe me, I've done my share of 'resting' in my time. Only nothing so civilized as busking—not where I came from. I was stuck with slinging hash and pearl diving. Doing waitress work—" I spelled it out for him, as he looked confused. "And washing dishes. The hours were rotten, the tips were lousy, and it was a toss-up which was going to cave in first, your feet or your back. But it was honest work and I earned an honest dollar. I'm not ashamed of it and neither should you be."

"I'm not, really," he said. "It's just that, it may be honest, but it isn't quite legal. They have laws about busking in the Underground. There are heavy fines if we get caught."

"Don't worry. I'm not going to go around telling anybody." It was now clear why Des had refused to tell Heyhoe where he was working the other night. The rigmarole about Arab parties *was* better than admitting to illegal busking in the Tube. If Heyhoe knew that Des was breaking one law, he would assume that Des would break any and all laws.

"No," Des said. "You wouldn't, would you? You're not that sort."

"Play something else for me." I wasn't fool enough to insult him by opening my purse. "I'd love to hear some more. You just about had me dancing down the corridor."

"Right you are!" He raised the clarinet to his lips, winked at me and swung into *I'm Looking for a Man with a Heart of Gold*, the *Gold Diggers'* theme song.

Well, I know a cue when I hear one. I hiked up my skirt and went into the old routine.

Suddenly, we had an audience. I had been dimly aware of a roaring sound in the distance. It seemed that a train had come into the station and disgorged its passengers. Some of them hurried past, but a lot of them stopped to watch.

"Hey—look at the old girl go!" It could have been better phrased, I thought, but it didn't stop me. I was caught up in the music and the dance.

"Jeez!" a tourist said. "They make their grandmothers work with them in this country?"

I could still do it. I high-kicked his silly hat off.

There was a burst of laughter and applause. A shower of coins rained on the sacking. The incautious one retrieved his hat and came up grinning—he tossed a pound coin into the kitty.

"Let me through, please—" Someone on the edge of the crowd began pushing to the front.

"Oh-oh, watch it!" someone warned.

"Transport police!" Des broke off abruptly. "Let's get out of here!"

"The money—" I bent to gather up our takings, as Des pulled at me. I got most of it gathered up in the sack before he won the tug-of-war.

"Come on!" He gripped me, I held tight to the sack and we ran, jingling, towards another roaring sound in the distance. Behind us, pounding footsteps pursued.

Again, we were caught up in endless corridors, the footsteps drew nearer. My legs were weakening, there was a stitch in my side, I could not catch my breath properly.

"I can't—" I gasped. "I can't run any more. You go ahead—let him catch me. I don't care."

"Right." Des did not slacken his pace nor let go of my arm. "You want me to tell Martha to come down and bail you out at the Magistrates' Court in the morning?"

He'd said the magic words. Suddenly, my second wind came through. Now I was ahead of him, racing down the flight of stairs.

Ahead of us, the doors of the waiting train began to slide shut. We put on one final burst of speed, Des wedged his shoulder against one door and held it while I slipped through.

Des let the doors slam shut, the train began to move, and we collapsed into seats as the baleful face of the transport policeman receded.

"We made it!" I crowed. "and I've still got all the money. Look!" I jingled the sack at him.

"Hey—great!" He threw his arms around me and we hugged and giggled wildly.

"You were terrific!" he said.

"So were you!"

We began to notice that we were getting some very peculiar sidelong glances from our fellow passengers, but that just made us giggle harder. Des tootled his clarinet at them, but we were laughing too much and he couldn't play it properly.

"We change here." The train slid to a stop at the next station and we got out, doubtless to the great relief of the other passengers.

After that, it was clear sailing until we got to St. John's Wood.

CHAPTER 16

"And where have you been all this time?" Evangeline demanded.

"Mother, we've been worried sick. You might have let us know—"

"I left a note," I pointed out indignantly. "What more did you want—hourly bulletins?"

"They wouldn't have come amiss," Evangeline said. "And it might have kept you in touch with what was going on here. While you've been kicking up your heels all over London—"

I kept my face blank. She couldn't possibly know how close to the mark she'd come.

"—we've had quite a day. The police were back."

"They wanted to know where you were," Martha said ominously. "And we couldn't tell them."

"Good." It had obviously been the right day to disappear. In retrospect, I'd had an even better day than I'd thought.

"Well," Martha said, "where *were* you?"

"Oh, here, there and everywhere." With my most innocent expression, I pulled out the programmes for the matinee and evening shows and tossed them on the table. "I've been catching up with some West End productions."

"Not a bad alibi," Evangeline said judiciously. "I suppose you also have the ticket stubs, and you were undoubtedly chatty enough with the box-office people and the programme sellers so that they'd remember you?"

"Undoubtedly." I used my innocent smile this time. It cut no ice. "So you've had a busy day with the police, have you?"

"Indeed, and furthermore—" Perhaps Evangeline had taken my earlier comments to heart, she no longer sounded like Ethel Barrymore in the last stages of despair.

"Furthermore—" She was now using a straight documen-

133

tary Voice of Doom. "We have had Juanita flinging a
fandango all over the place all day."

"Well, it's her house," I said. "Or her grandson's."

"That's part of the problem," Martha said. "The police
took Jasper away as soon as he got home from the office.
They said they wanted him to help with inquiries—but he
hasn't come back yet."

"Oh!" That was serious. "But I thought they'd cleared
him of any involvement with Mick's death."

"It wasn't Mick they were inquiring about this time."
Evangeline carefully avoided my eyes. "Anni is still missing . . . and it seems that they've pulled a body out of the
canal recently . . ."

"Oh!" That was even worse.

"Yes. And, since Jasper owns the house and is older than
the others, they took him to look at the body and see if he
could identify it as Anni's."

"Oh!" No wonder he wasn't back yet. He'd be lucky if he
was out by New Year. No matter which way that cat decided
to jump, he was for it. If he told the truth and identified the
body as Fiona's, he'd opened a whole new can of beans and
they'd be questioning him for days yet. If he decided to lie
and claimed that it was Anni's body, he was still going to
have a lot of explaining to do.

"Exactly," Evangeline said grimly.

"Oh! Oh dear . . ."

"For heaven's sake, stop saying 'Oh!' Mother! Can't you
see how appalling this situation is?"

"Oh yes," I said. If Martha could see half of what I was
seeing, she'd be on the next plane back to Los Angeles—
police permission or not.

"I thought I heard the front door—" Juanita came into
the drawing-room and looked around eagerly. She saw me
and her face fell—more than usual, that is. "Oh, it's you."

"Sorry—" I apologized.

"Pah!" she spat and turned on her heel.

Evangeline rolled her eyes at me, obviously close to the
end of her tether.

"I warn you—" Juanita spun on her heel anad faced us
again. "If anything happens to my grandson, I shall wreak
such vengeance as the world has never known!"

"*Dear* Juanita, that always was one of your best lines. Why don't you save it until morning and give Superintendent Hi-de-Ho the benefit of it?"

"Pah!" She exited, leaving silence behind her as we waited uneasily to see if she was going to take an encore.

"Sometimes," Evangeline said at last, "one wonders whether one has underestimated dear Beau's patience—or his stupidity."

Across the hallway, a door slammed.

"I can't stand much more of this," Martha said tearfully. "Mother, can't we go home?" She was quivering with nerves.

"Why don't you go to bed?" I suggested. "Things will look better in the morning."

"I can't!" Martha wailed. "That awful woman has taken my room again!"

"Then go upstairs and take hers!" I snapped.

"Oh no, I couldn't do that. Jasper might come back."

"So what? Even if he does, you don't think he's going to try to climb into bed with his grandmother, do you?"

"Mother!" She couldn't even take a joke.

How had it happened? Despite her age, Martha and the Permissive Society had missed all contact. She was a throwback to a Victorian generation. Or was it some basic insecurity? Was it because she had never had a father around during the vital years? It wasn't really my fault. I had divorced twice and been widowed once. Not a bad record, as Hollywood records go. Still, with Evangeline's censorious gaze on me, I felt guilty.

"Oh, all right," I said. "You can take *my* room and *I'll* go upstairs."

"Mother, you can't!" But Martha cheered up immediately.

"Why not? If Jasper isn't back by now, it's highly unlikely he'll be back tonight . . ."

I was less brave as I entered the *terra incognita* of Jasper's flat. It was not until the doorknob turned under my hand and I was able to walk in that it occurred to me that possibly the flat should have been locked.

On the other hand, Juanita had been flouncing in and out of the flat all day, so perhaps it wasn't surprising. She was great at slamming doors; I doubted that she was so good at locking them.

Half-expecting to be challenged, I moved through the shadowed flat. The lights seemed dimmer than the lights downstairs. The layout was different, somehow, more old-fashioned, despite the more modern furniture. It occurred to me that this was probably the way our flat had looked before the extensive renovations.

This was a good adequate flat, but no one would ever mistake it for a love-nest.

That expression again—why did it keep teasing at the corner of my mind?

I opened the wrong door on a masculine room in terminal disarray which looked even worse because of the unmade bed. I snapped off the light and shut the door again quickly.

The next door obviously opened into the right room. I could smell Juanita's perfume and did not appreciate it. Opening the window would take care of that.

The light revealed a room nearly as slovenly as Jasper's— he came by it honestly, it seemed. This bed, too, was unmade. Evidently, the landlord didn't get his own flat serviced—which seemed a bit odd.

Of more concern to me at the moment was the sudden distaste I felt about slipping between those rumpled sheets.

I opened the window and let the room begin to air while I thought it over. I would feel silly about retreating downstairs again—anyway, it wouldn't do any good, there was no bed for me and Martha would just have something more to complain about.

The day was catching up with me and I was so tired I could have slept on a picket fence. I would have preferred a clean picket fence, but life is a series of compromises, anyway.

The room smelled fresher now, if damper. Most of the lingering traces of the cloying scent clung to the pillows. I stripped off the pillowcases and the bottom sheet and dropped them in an untidy (it was catching) heap just outside the bedroom door. Then I tucked the top sheet down firmly and let the blanket serve as the second sheet.

It was only marginally more satisfactory than that picket

fence, but I was too tired to be choosy. I closed the window and fell into bed. I was asleep almost as soon as my head touched the pillow.

At first I thought I was having another nightmare. Then I thought vaguely that it was an action replay of my awakening the other morning—but that wasn't quite right, either. At least I had been getting second-hand air then; none at all was reaching me now. Something soft and smothering was being pressed down over my face . . . Finally, my groggy brain snapped to alertness—almost too late.

Someone was trying to kill me!

I pushed at the pillow covering my face, but the person bending over me, holding it down firmly, was prepared for that feeble struggle.

I began to fight back furiously in the only way I could, taking my attacker by surprise. Thank heaven for my dancer's muscles! I drew my legs up and lashed out with them, catching someone in the stomach.

The pressure on the pillow disappeared and I hurled it away from me. Now I could hear someone scrabbling across the floor towards the door, panting for breath.

Or was that me? I was drawing in great lungfuls of air, not silently at all. I fumbled for the lamp switch, but the door opened and closed before I found it. When the light went on, my assailant was gone. I decided to quit while I was ahead—I wasn't going to chase him.

I staggered over to the window and opened it wide, leaning out into a night that had unexpectedly become clear and crisp. A bright moon illuminated the garden beneath.

A full moon—was that the answer? Why else would anyone want to kill me? It must have been a lunatic. A homicidal lunatic, triggered off by the night of the full moon.

It had happened like that in *Moon Without Mercy*. For a moment it seemed quite possible, reasonable, even.

Then the oxygen began clearing my brain and a more logical explanation sprang into it: everyone had known Juanita was using this room, someone was trying to kill *her*.

They'd have had a good chance of succeeding, too. You

could tell just by looking at her that she hadn't kept herself
in shape. She'd let her muscles go flabby and put on too
much fat—she would never have been able to fight off the
attacker the way I had.

It must have been a nasty shock for someone when I
kicked them across the room. Almost as nasty as the shock I
had had when I came back to consciousness to find that
pillow over my face.

Suddenly I was shivering, and it wasn't just from the cold
night air. I wanted—I needed—human warmth and com-
panionship. And I didn't care if I damned well *did* disturb
everyone in the house. Someone wasn't sleeping anyway.

"Don't be absurd, Trixie," Evangeline said coldly.
"You've had a nightmare, that's all."

It was infuriating. I had no proof that I had been
attacked—not even a bruise to display. If the killer had
succeeded and removed the pillow before anyone found me
in the morning, there was every good chance that it would
have been written off as a natural death.

As for Juanita—in the shape she was in, there would have
been no doubt at all.

"Oh, Mother—" I had tried to be quiet, but Evangeline
had begun making such a fuss that she had wakened
Martha. "Mother, you might have been killed!"

"That's right," Evangeline said. "I *told* you to let Martha
have that room."

Martha and I both looked at her suspiciously.

"Just as well I didn't—" Against my better judgement, I
gave her the benefit of the doubt. "Martha's muscles aren't
in much better state than Juanita's."

Evangeline flicked up her eyebrows in that way that
meant "Precisely"; fortunately, Martha missed that.

"Really, Mother, I'm younger and stronger than you—"

"But you haven't her rat-like cunning. If any of us had to
be in that room, your mother was the best possible choice.
However—" Evangeline abruptly remembered her earlier,
more comforting stance. "However, I don't believe a word
of it. I think she just had a very realistic nightmare. Night
terrors, I believe they're called."

Someday I might have another serious go at trying to kill

her. I wondered suddenly if the feeling was mutual. Was it remotely possible that it had been Evangeline who had sneaked up the stairs and into my room and held that pillow over my face?

No. Sanity reasserted itself. If it had been Evangeline I had sent flying, she would never have recovered so fast. Nor was she strong enough physically to have borne down on the pillow with that relentless pressure that had almost finished me.

"Listen!" I held up my hand for silence and we could hear stealthy sounds in the hall outside.

"He's trying to get away!" With reinforcements, I was ready to give chase. "Let's go get him!"

Martha trailed behind us, whimpering protests as we rushed silently to the hall door and flung it open.

"Stay where you are!" Evangeline roared. "I have a gun!"

"Don't shoot!" a terrified voice pleaded. "It's all right. It's only me."

"Martha, get the lights!" I ordered.

For once, she did as she was told without protest. There was a click and the hall flooded with light. Hugh Carpenter stood frozen at the foot of the stairs.

"Please, put the gun away," he begged. He'd believe anything of Evangeline. "Why—" He blinked in the light as the truth registered. "Why, you haven't got a gun at all."

"Oh," Evangeline said flatly. "It's *you*. I might have known it."

"What—?" The door opposite opened and Juanita filled the doorway, looking like the Phantom of the Opera after a bad night. "What is going on here? Why have we a crowd scene in the front hall in the middle of the night?"

"Please, let's all keep calm," Hugh said desperately. "I'm sorry I roused the house, we were trying not to disturb anyone. I've just driven Jasper home from the police station; they've just released him."

"A likely story!" Evangeline snorted. "Where is he? Produce him!"

"Here I am." Jasper appeared at the top of the stairs. He had obviously entered silently earlier. It had been Hugh who had stumbled and given the game away.

"My baby!" Juanita possessed a good turn of speed for her

age and condition. She raced up the stairs and entwined herself around the embarrassed Jasper. "My *pobrecito!* Are you all right? Did they hurt you? We will sue them for false arrest!"

"I wasn't arrested," Jasper said. "I was just helping with inquiries."

"*Pah!* That is what they always announce officially—just before they slam the cell door! They are liars and—"

Jasper swayed against his grandmother, going paler than ever.

"Take it easy, old man." Hugh bounded up the stairs to take the weight from Juanita. "Look—" he appealed to us, "this lad's been through enough tonight. Let him get to bed now. You can continue this in the morning."

"But what happened?" Juanita clung to Jasper as Hugh tried to detach her. "You must tell me. That girl—it was Anni, yes? That is why you are so shocked. You identified the body?"

"Yes—" Jasper said—"but it wasn't Anni." He gave his grandmother a guilty secretive look. "It was Fiona."

There was a strange silence.

"Who's Fiona?" Evangeline remembered that we weren't supposed to know.

Everyone ignored the question. Hugh caught Jasper around the shoulders and bundled him into his room.

Juanita descended the stairs slowly with an air of preoccupied satisfaction. A secret smile twisted her uneven lips.

I had the sudden conviction that she knew about Fiona—and she knew a lot more than we did.

CHAPTER 17

"It should be obvious to the meanest intelligence," Evangeline said. "It was Jasper who tried to kill you last night, under the impression that you were his grandmother."

"If anyone caught you saying that, Jasper could sue you for everything up to and including your back teeth. Jasper is practically the only person in the house with an alibi—he was at the police station all night."

"Was he? Just remember, he appeared at the *top* of the stairs. Who knows how long he'd been up there."

"But Hugh had just brought him home."

"So he says, but you know how long it takes Hugh to park his car. There could well have been ample time for Jasper to slip upstairs and try to kill you before Hugh came blundering in and roused the house."

"I hate to say it, Mother—" Martha poured more coffee all around. "But she might be right. There's another point: Juanita was still in that room when Jasper left for the police station, he wouldn't have known we'd all changed rooms again while he was gone."

"I'm sure it couldn't have taken Hugh that long to park at that hour of the night—morning." But there was another pertinent fact I wasn't going to encourage them by mentioning. Those pillowcases and that sheet heaped just outside the bedroom door and reeking of Juanita's scent would have led anyone to believe that she was still there. In the darkness, the heap of laundry would not have been distinguishable as such, but the spoor from it would have convinced anyone that they had come to the right room.

"Hugh isn't that clumsy," Martha went off on a tangent suddenly. "He's just so abrupt sometimes that he seems awkward."

"Hmmph!" Evangeline was always ready for a sparring match. "That man could have more legs than a centipede and he'd still wind up with every foot crammed into his mouth!"

"That's unfair! Just because you don't like him, you—"

I tiptoed away and left them to it. Interesting though I found Martha's defence of Hugh, it would probably come to nothing. There had been other lame ducks over the years, but she had always elected to remain with the one she considered lamest of all—me. How did I get so lucky?

It was too much to hope for to be able to sneak away again today, but I decided to give it the old college try. I dressed rapidly and got as far as the front door. Then I made a major mistake: I opened it.

Detective-Superintendent Heyhoe stood there, his finger poised to ring the doorbell.

"Good morning, madam," he said nastily. "Going somewhere, were we?"

"I was just absconding to Honolulu with the Widows' and Orphans' Fund," I said. "How about you?"

Detective-Sergeant Singer snickered, earning black looks from both of us.

"We thought we'd make a few more inquiries," Heyhoe said. "Now that we have a bit more to inquire about."

"Have you?" I asked innocently. "You do start early in the morning, don't you?"

"You never can tell what the early bird will catch. May we come in?"

When it comes from a policeman, how do you say no to a request like that? I stepped back and they moved into the hallway.

"You want the upstairs flat, I suppose." I tried to plant the suggestion in their minds.

"Now why should you suppose that? As long as we're downstairs, we might as well start here. The others are up, I trust?"

"In the kitchen, finishing breakfast. Would you like some coffee?"

"Coffee?" The door opposite opened and Juanita stepped out. "Good! I could use some." She paused to bestow an automatic smirk on the two male strangers, then lost no time heading for the kitchen.

"Who was that?" Heyhoe was reeling visibly. Juanita was

no sight for anyone of a sensitive disposition first thing in the morning.

I toyed with saying, "I never saw her before in my life—I thought she was with you," but he was in no mood for games.

"That's Jasper's grandmother," I said. "She's rushed up to Town to defend what seems to be the only cub in the litter."

"You mean—" Now Detective-Sergeant Singer was reeling. "You mean *that's* Juanita Morez? Beauregard Sylvester's wife?"

"Come along, Singer," Heyhoe said impatiently, having been the first to recover. He led the way down the hall, gave a perfunctory tap and threw open the kitchen door.

"Oh, it's you, Hoo-Hay," Evangeline said wearily. "*Now* what?"

"That's Heyhoe, madam."

"What's in a name?"

"Quite so, madam. Perhaps you wouldn't mind a few more questions?"

"Haven't we answered enough already?"

"In the light of information received, we find it necessary to reopen inquiries."

"Who *is* this man?" Juanita demanded.

"This is the policeman—" Evangeline had no compunction about unleashing her on him—"who kept dear Jasper at the police station all night."

"*You* did that?" Juanita advanced on him dangerously, every wattle quivering with fury. "*Pah!* I spit on you—and your questions!"

"As you wish, madam." Buster Keaton couldn't have kept a deader pan. "Nevertheless, inquiries must be pursued."

Detective-Sergeant Singer unlimbered his notepad and stood waiting.

"Martha," I said, "please pour the gentlemen some coffee." They did not object and, for a wonder, Martha obeyed without argument.

"*Dear* Trixie—" Evangeline swept me with a glance that took in my hat, coat—and intentions. "You were on your way out. You mustn't let us keep you."

She wanted to get rid of me. She didn't trust what I

might reveal—and she was right. I had no objections to
getting out of the way myself.

"That's right." I began sidling towards the door. 'I'll be
getting along—"

"Just a moment, madam." Heyhoe barred my way. "We'd
like a few words before you go."

I didn't need Evangeline's warning glance to tell me that
I had to be very careful.

"Fiona Jones," Heyhoe said abruptly. "What do you know
about her."

"Nothing," I answered, adding with perfect truth, "I
never met her. Who is she?"

"Was she someone we met at the Press Reception or
Premiere?" Evangeline asked helpfully. "One meets so
many people at these parties—the names and faces all blur
together."

"I don't think you'd have met her there, madam. She
hasn't been to many parties recently."

Juanita had gone very quiet. No longer projecting
righteous fury, she had retreated to the farthest chair and
blanked out all personality. She could have been a disem-
bodied spirit, just barely visible, as she sat there sipping
her coffee. If Heyhoe had been more astute, he would have
realized immediately that he was questioning the wrong
people.

As it was, it took him several more questions before he
began to notice something odd about the atmosphere. He
paused in mid-question and lifted his head, sniffing almost
audibly, like an old hound catching the scent.

Which was just what had happened. Juanita had shifted
position suddenly, sending a shock wave of scent across the
table. Her scent had more presence than she had—and it
wasn't going to take the greatest brain in the Universe to
wonder why.

Evangeline had been casting sidelong glances in Juanita's
direction for the past few minutes.

Juanita raised her coffee cup and tried to hide behind it
as she realized that every eye was upon her. For once, she
did not appreciate being in the limelight.

"Mrs. Sylvester—" Heyhoe spoke with deceptive gentle-
ness, perhaps remembering that she and Beauregard had

paid a great deal in taxes over the years. "Mrs. Sylvester, what do you know about your grandson's liaison with Fiona Jones?"

"It is not true!" Juanita flared. "He had nothing to do with that girl!"

"Really? His friends seem to think otherwise. Perhaps he kept it a secret from you, knowing that you would not approve."

"There are no secrets between us!"

It was as unlikely a story as any I had ever heard and, obviously, Heyhoe felt the same.

"Quite so, madam," he said flatly. "Nevertheless, the consensus of opinion appears to be—"

"*That* for your consensus!" Juanita hurled the contents of her coffee cup into his face and charged from the room while we all stood frozen.

The trouble with real life is that there is no Director to shout, "Cut", and tidy up the action between shots. Heyhoe stood there, with coffee dripping from his jowls; Singer lowered his notebook and stared at him aghast. Martha sprang for a tea-towel and began mopping down Heyhoe—a gesture he did not appreciate. He snatched the towel from her and dabbed furiously at his face. Whatever else, Juanita had just forfeited her status as a respected taxpayer and joined the rest of us felons.

"I have a fearful headache," Evangeline announced firmly. "I'm going back to bed."

"I'm afraid I still have a few more questions, madam."

"You can speak to me later." Evangeline continued her stately progress towards the door. "I'm far too ill right now."

"I can either ask them here, madam, or I shall be obliged to require you to accompany me to the station and answer them there."

"You wouldn't dare!"

Anyone else would have known better than to speak to a senior police official like that. Anyone but Evangeline.

In *The Happy Couple* series, everyone from the local patrolman to the Commissioner of Police had caved in when she faced them with flashing eyes and imperious manner. Heyhoe just seemed to grow two feet taller; his eyes and voice turned to steel.

"Sergeant, have the car brought round," he ordered.

"No, please—" Martha tried to intercede. "You can't do that. She's old—she doesn't understand. She doesn't know what she's saying. She doesn't mean it."

"Are you suggesting I'm mentally incompetent?" Evangeline snapped. "I can assure you I mean every word I've ever uttered—especially to Hay-Hee here."

"I never doubted that you did, madam." Heyhoe's face was grim. "That's why we're going to continue this little session at the station."

"You ought to be ashamed of yourself!" Martha railed. "Haven't you got anything better to do that run around harassing old ladies?"

"Just come along now, madam." He ignored Martha.

"If you persist in this ridiculous course of action—" Evangeline threatened. "I won't solve your case for you."

"I wasn't aware that I was relying on you to do so, madam." Now she'd done it; he was livid with rage.

"Look—" I tried to distract him. "This *is* ridiculous. Martha is right—you should have better things to do. Why aren't you out looking for Anni? She and Mick were lovers—everybody knows that makes her the most likely suspect. Now she's disappeared. She must have run away because she killed him."

"Possibly, madam. But why should she have killed him?"

"Because he knew she'd killed Fiona! Maybe he was even the cause of it. I'll bet he made a pass at Fiona—or vice versa—and Anni caught them at it. In Jasper's flat. Then there was that struggle—heaven knows there was enough noise. Of course," I admitted, "it's possible Fiona's death was an accident. She may have hit her head when she fell and it was more fatal than it would have been for someone else—she seemed to bruise easily. But Mick got rid of the body—because he was doing it for Anni—"

"Trixie, shut up!" But not even Ethel Barrymore at her most thunderous could stop me now.

"After that, Anni decided she had to kill him, too, because he knew what she'd done and he was basically too honest not to tell someone eventually. She thought he was the only one who knew Fiona was dead. She didn't know we knew—"

"Indeed, madam? Neither did I."

"Mother, what are you saying?"

"I told you to shut up, Trixie!"

"Ladies, ladies—" Heyhoe was almost genial, now that things were going his way. "Be calm, ladies. We're *all* going to go down to the station now and sort this out."

"Not Martha," I said quickly. "She doesn't know a thing about it. She didn't arrive until it was all over."

"Ah?" Heyhoe was less than devastated at the news that Martha's presence was unnecessary. "Perhaps not Martha, then. We can always speak to her later." He began herding us towards the front door.

"Don't say anything more until I get there with a lawyer, Mother!" Martha followed us, shrieking instructions. "I'll call Hugh—"

"Oh, fine," Evangeline muttered. "That will be a great help!"

CHAPTER 18

If I should live for another thousand years, I never want to have another day like that one.

Oh, the police were perfectly polite, charming, even. They poured tea into us until it was squirting out of our ears. They were patient, courteous—and relentless. By the time I had answered the same questions sixteen times, I couldn't have lied, even if I'd wanted to. Which I didn't.

Evangeline could get as mad as she liked, but it was high time Heyhoe knew the truth. Not that I knew whether she was still mad, or not. They had separated us almost as soon as we arrived at the police station and put us into different rooms. After all, it had become pretty much of a blur as various policemen took turns questioning me.

By the time they let us go, I felt like the victim in a science-fiction movie. One of those losers who'd been strung up by their heels on a meat hook and systematically drained of blood and desinewed to provide sustenance for some vampiric monster from Outer Space.

Evangeline and I slumped in opposite corners of the back seat of the police car and didn't even speak to each other. With luck, she might never speak to me again—but I knew I couldn't count on that kind of luck.

Nor, probably, could I count on Martha's having been locked up permanently. At one point I had heard her shrieking and Hugh bleating outside my interrogation room. Their voices had risen to an uncomfortable pitch of arrogance and demand—then, unaccountably, fallen silent. After a few minutes, it had become clear that, whatever else had happened, the rescue bid had failed.

The police car swerved into the carriageway and drew up at the foot of the steps. Detective-Sergeant Singer leaped merrily out of the front seat and came round to open the door for us. Ah, youth! He was as fresh as he had been first thing this morning. He held the door open as two bedraggled wrecks crept past him.

"I'll see you later," he said to Evangeline, who surprised me.

Instead of snapping, "Not if I see you first," she nodded.

"Come for after-dinner drinks, dear boy," she invited. "We can discuss our little project then."

"Very good." He gave her an intimate look and patted his notebook pocket. Was he concealing evidence for her?

She was scheming again and it was more than I could bear. I went up the steps and left them to it. I was feeling too exhausted—too old—to try to cope with her. I could feel myself slowing down, each step seemed too high to mount . . .

"Twixie!" The front door flew open. "Oh, thank goodness! We've been wowwied sick!" Gwenda rushed down the steps to hug me, nearly knocking me over. Then, arm around my waist, she half-carried me up the remaining steps.

When I turned at the top, Evangeline was still lollygagging with Detective-Sergeant Singer. She had obviously not been put through as much of a wringer as I had—and the thought annoyed me. However, with Gwenda babbling happily beside me, it was hard not to look on the bright side.

"Has Martha come back yet?"

"No, she went out wight after you did and I haven't seen her since. Hugh was going to meet her at the police station and I haven't seen him, either."

"Oh well, they'll be along eventually." I could guarantee it. Nothing was going to keep Martha away for very long. No matter how much she had annoyed the police, there was a limit to what they could do about it. I thought wistfully of a nice Court case where a Judge could sentence someone to a term in prison for Contempt of Court. No doubt the police had been equally wistful.

"Do you think we should wing the police station and find out what's happened?"

"I'd rather not know." I followed her into the front hall. Evangeline was now climbing the steps behind us, leaning heavily on the wrought-iron railing.

Juanita's door remained closed, for which I was profoundly grateful. I had had enough for one day.

"Come upstairs," Gwenda urged. "I'll make tea—high
tea. You must be wavenous."

"Not tea." I shuddered. "I couldn't face another cup.
Come to think of it, I can't face any more stairs, either. Why
don't we all go out to dinner?" That would also postpone the
evil moment when I would have to face Martha.

"Oh!" Her face lit up. "That would be—"

"Nonsense!" Evangeline had come up behind us. "I'm far
too tired to go trailing out again to some restaurant. We'll
telephone one of those catering services and have meals
brought to us. It will be quicker and easier. Of course you'll
join us, my dear," she added to Gwenda. "Perhaps you
could recommend the best caterer."

"Oh yes," Gwenda said. "Don't wowwy about a thing. I'll
take care of it for you. Do you want Italian, Indian,
English—or Chinese again?"

"English," we chorused firmly.

Juanita's door opened and my heart sank. We should have
known better than to stand discussing food in the entrance
hall. It was the one sure way to smoke her out.

"Oh!" Ursula stood in the doorway, clutching an armload
of towels and bed linen. "I didn't realize anyone was out
here. I was just—" She broke off in confusion.

"Just what?" Evangeline demanded.

"Well . . . servicing the flats," Ursula admitted. "It's
Anni's job, really, but since she isn't around, we can't leave
our guests with unmade beds and dirty towels."

"Anni's job . . ." Evangeline was thoughtful. "Does
Haw-Hee know that?"

"I don't think so." Ursula shrugged. "I don't see why our
domestic arrangements need concern him."

"Quite right," Evangeline approved; she loved the idea
that she might know something Heyhoe didn't. "And it's
very kind of you to concern yourself with our comfort.
We're just sending out for dinner, you must join us."

"Why, thank you," Ursula said hesitantly, "I'd like that. I
must just put this in the laundry basket first." She turned
and started up the stairs, stopped half way and turned back.
"You're sure—?"

"Quite sure," Evangeline said. "We'll be delighted to have you."

Ursula gave her a shy half-smile, turned and vanished up the stairs. Gwenda was perhaps less delighted to have a rival for our attention, but followed us into the flat with good grace and began telephoning our orders while we went to our rooms to freshen up.

The rooms were neat and tidy, beds made and all surfaces sparkling—as they had been all along, both pre- and post-Anni. Remembering the state of Jasper's flat, I realized that Ursula was only extending her courtesy services to us and not to her landlord. Presumably, she drew the line at taking over Anni's chores completely. It was neighbourly enough of her to take care of us—after all, she'd been working hard all day.

Evangeline repaired her make-up, humming under her breath, and I remembered something else.

"Just what," I asked suspiciously, "have you got going with Sergeant Singer? I should think you'd never want to see him again after today. Why have you invited him round this evening?"

"He's a dear boy, really," Evangeline said absently. "He may have to earn a living in the police force, but his heart is in the right place—the cinema."

"How nice." Maybe I'd feel better after some food, but I was in a nasty mood right now. "What a pity the parade's gone by. He'd better stick with the police, there's more of a future in it."

"Oh, I don't know. . . ." Evangeline was being maddening again. "There are still opportunities—if one knows where to look."

"I hope he isn't thinking of looking to Beau. You told me he was on the verge of bankruptcy."

"That was several days ago," Evangeline said complacently. "I gather the situation is improving by the hour. Several more floors of Cinema City have been rented since all the publicity began."

"You can't mean it! After all *that* publicity?"

"Trixie, you know perfectly well that there's no such thing as bad publicity—so long as they spell your name right." Evangeline leaned into the mirror and applied fresh lipstick. "In *our* business, at least. I'm not so sure Jasper's stockbrokerage is entirely happy about developments. But—" she blotted the lipstick—"that's *his* problem."

"I'm beginning to feel sorry for poor Jasper. His family must be a sore trial to him—and now his friends aren't proving much better."

"If you ask me—" Evangeline wore her Hanging Judge's face again.

"I didn't—and don't you dare accuse that poor boy of being a murderer again!"

Dinner was delicious. The girls were charming company and, perhaps best of all, Martha and Hugh continued to be absent. The party spirit only began to fade when the doorbell rang and Sergeant Singer joined us.

Evangeline poured brandy with a lavish hand. "Trot, trot, trot," I murmured under my breath as she handed me my snifter.

"Dear Trixie has already looked too enthusiastically upon the grape," she told the puzzled Singer, casting a poisonous look in my direction.

"Surely not," he said gallantly, raising his own snifter to me.

Evangeline sniffed.

"Well . . ." Like a sleek cat scenting trouble, Ursula rose and prepared to escape. "I can't thank you enough for such a lovely evening and delicious meal, but I'm afraid I still have some work to do. It's been *so* nice to meet you socially—" She smiled upon the bemused Singer.

"My pleasure entirely." He sprang to his feet and hurried to open the door for her. "Miss Sinclair has told me about your restoration work. Perhaps some day you'd allow me to—"

"Of course. Just ring me—you *do* have all our telephone numbers." Ursula had claws, after all.

She made as neat an exit as any she had ever edited. Singer returned to his chair and Evangeline had the nerve to look expectantly at Gwenda. That was too much— Gwenda was *my* guest.

"I can't tell you," I said, as Gwenda looked to me uncertainly, "how nice it is to be at home with my friends

around me." Sergeant Singer could interpret that any way
he chose. "Is Des still at work? We should ask him down to
join us. Yes—" I was feeling more expansive by the
moment. "Yes—and Juanita, too. Let's have a party. Why
not?"

"Why not, indeed?" Evangeline's eyes narrowed, but she
wasn't as annoyed as I'd hoped she'd be. Was I playing into
her hands?

"It's past midnight—" Gwenda glanced at her watch.
"Des should be coming home any minute now. But do you
think we should disturb Mrs. Sylvester this late?"

"As I recall her habits—" Evangeline wrinkled her nose
in distaste—"the lateness of the hour would only add to the
occasion for her. I'm surprised she hasn't tried to gatecrash
us already. It's most unlike her to stay away when food and
drink are circulating."

"It is, isn't it?" Gwenda was vaguely uneasy. "Do you
think she's all wight?"

"Perhaps we ought to check." Sergeant Singer was
suddenly alert and half way out of his chair.

"Oh no, I forgot—" Gwenda relaxed. "Ursula wouldn't
have been servicing her flat if she was there. And I didn't
hear her come in later, did you? She must be out."

"The only reasonable explanation." Evangeline still
frowned. "But . . . out where? She refuses to be seen in
public. And I don't have the feeling that she and Beau are
so close these days that she'd be spending a domestic
evening with him . . ."

"No—" Gwenda giggled abruptly. "He's not the domestic
type." She glanced around the flat. "Not unless he's playing
house."

"Is that so?" Singer was almost as interested as Evangeline. I had already surmised something of the sort, of
course. This flat was too much of a stage set.

"Oh yes," Gwenda babbled artlessly—or was it? There
was a familiar echo in her performance—I might have been
watching myself when young. "It's vewy useful, having a
house in your gwandson's name. There's usually been a
mystewious lady tucked away down here. That's why we
were so wiveted to get inside and see the place—especially
since it was wefurbished a few weeks ago. It was a gweat

joke with us. We talked about taking bets on the next inhabitant. Anni said, at the wate of turnover, one of us was due to be offered it soon."

"Really, my dear?" This time it was Evangeline who poured more drink into Gwenda's glass. Sergeant Singer had settled back and his hand was creeping towards his notebook. "But surely, *you* wouldn't be interested?"

"Cwumbs, no! But I wasn't too sure about Anni sometimes. She's been having a bad time wecently, that's why she cleaned the flats instead of paying went. If she got an offer, I couldn't swear she'd wefuse. Especially as things hadn't been going well with her and Mick. And there's a persistent wumour that Beau may twy for a no-fault divorce. If he did that, Anni said, he'd be up for gwabs."

"Would he?" Evangeline continued questioning, obviously having picked up some points this afternoon. Sergeant Singer was unobtrusively taking notes. "But was Anni going to do the grabbing? Or Fiona?"

"Cwumbs! I never thought of that!" Head to one side, Gwenda considered it for a moment. "You know, it could be. Jasper was never as affectionate with Fiona as with his other girls. P'waps that was because she wasn't weally his girl, at all."

"I think we're getting somewhere," Evangeline said with satisfaction. "Juanita must have known all this—or suspected a good part of it. She always kept a closer eye on Beau than he realized. Even in Hollywood, she supported a couple of private eyes who spent all their time keeping tabs on Beau. I can remember the time . . ."

"Don't stop," Sergeant Singer said eagerly. "What do you remember?"

"That—" Evangeline had a reminiscent smile—"is hardly pertinent to this investigation."

"Ah . . ." With a disappointed sigh, Singer tried another tack. "Did Beau know he was under constant surveillance?"

"Sometimes he did, sometimes he didn't. Whenever he caught one of them following him, he had an almighty row with Juanita and she always swore she'd fire the agency and never do it again. Of course what really happened was that they'd just put a different agent on the job."

"And you think that was going on in this country, too?" Singer underlined his last notation.

"Does the leopard change its spots?" Evangeline glanced restively towards the door. "I don't believe she's out at all— she's just lying low because she knows we're catching up with her. Let's go and beard her in her den!"

Sergeant Singer was right behind her as she charged for the door. Gwenda and I sat where we were and stared at each other.

"Cwumbs! Does she go on like this all the time?"

"More often than not," I sighed. "This time there's a bit more substance to it but, basically, she's still playing the lead in *The Happy Couple*."

"Better that than the lead in *The Wevenge of the White Squaw*—Oh, cwumbs!" Gwenda clapped her hand over her mouth. "I didn't mean that. Not the way it sounded."

"Maybe not, but you could be right," I said thoughtfully. "Someone deliberately scalped Mick to throw suspicion on Evangeline—and Juanita always hated her. Maybe—" I heaved myself out of my chair. "Maybe we'd better get across the hall and find out what's going on."

CHAPTER 19

Sergeant Singer was still hammering on the door when we caught up with them.

"Break it down!" Evangeline urged ghoulishly. "She must be in there. She's hiding!"

"We can't—yet." Singer hammered again and reinforced this with a couple of kicks. He was looking increasingly worried. "Open up—" He gave voice, accompanied by another volley of knocks and kicks. "Open up—it's the police!"

The information did nothing towards getting the door opened.

"I told you we'll have to break it down," Evangeline said. "Back off—" She began issuing directions. "Run at it and slam it with your shoulder for all you're worth."

"I don't believe I have enough grounds for that, madam." For an instant, Singer sounded just like his superior. There was something of Heyhoe, too, in the carefully controlled look he shot at Evangeline. "This isn't America, you know."

"If you'll wait a minute," Gwenda said reasonably, "I'll go upstairs and get the key from Ursula."

"If you'd be so kind." Singer stepped away from the door gratefully. "That would be the best solution."

Gwenda was up the stairs and back in a flash with the key and a slightly puzzled expression. "Ursula isn't there," she reported, "but the key was hanging on the hook with the others."

"Thank you." Singer relieved her of it deftly and opened the door. We all crowded into the studio flat behind him. One quick look was enough to show us that it was empty.

"P'waps she's gone back to Jasper's flat," Gwenda suggested. "After all, Martha weally belongs in this woom."

"It would be most unlike her to be so cooperative,"

Evangeline said, "but I suppose it *is* remotely possible."
She led the way upstairs.

"I'll get Jasper's key." Gwenda darted ahead of us.

"Keys seem to be freely available in this house." Singer
made another note.

"They certainly are," I said bitterly, remembering the
way Martha had burst in on me. "And the flatmates aren't
shy about handing them out."

"Here you are." Gwenda returned with the key and
watched expectantly as Singer twisted it in the lock. He
beat her into the flat by a short head, then had to pause.

"Which room is hers?"

"That one." I pointed, surprised that he needed to ask.
The heavy scent still hung in the air, marking the spot like
an X. Perhaps she *had* returned to her grandson's flat. Then
I noticed a torn sheet kicked into the corner—that was the
source of the scent. It also answered the question I had
been pondering: no one had serviced Jasper's flat. The sheet
had been lying around since I had tossed it out of the
room—only it hadn't been torn then.

"Empty—" Evangeline's voice floated out of the room
and I moved forward to the doorway.

The room looked much as it had when I fled it so
precipitately. If anything, it was even untidier. Pieces of
crumpled paper scattered around never help. Singer bent
and picked up one of them, smoothing it out.

"What does it say?" Evangeline tried to read it over his
shoulder. When he blocked her view, she swooped and
captured one of her own. Gwenda and I did the same.

"'I'm sowwy'—" Gwenda read out. "That's all mine say."

"'Forgive me'—" Evangeline had had better luck. "'My
Latin blood overwhelmed me and I have brought disgrace
upon my family. I am taking the only honourable way
out'—"

"Cwumbs! They're suicide notes! How can we tell
Jasper?"

"There must be a fuller one—" Evangeline bent and
whisked the last piece of paper out from under Singer's
fingers. "One with a confession. She must be admitting to
the murders—otherwise, why should she kill herself? She'd
never do anything to please Beau."

"'He wanted Fiona—'" Singer gave up and read out his fragment of the jigsaw puzzle. "'So she had to die. Thus perish all who try to steal what is mine.'"

"Cwumbs! She'd have her work cut out for her if she twied to kill all Beau's mistwesses!"

"But it doesn't make sense," I protested. "Why all these scrappy notes? Why not just one?"

"She was probably working out her thoughts," Singer said. "Some suicides do that. They think they'll make an outline, then combine their entire rationale into one long dignified letter, only their problems overwhelm them before they finish and they rush out and do what they were intending to do all along."

"'I always wanted to play *Anna Karenina*—'" I contributed.

"We are not interested in your unrealistic aspirations at this late stage, Trixie." Evangeline was severe.

"No, no! That's what my note says." I waved it at them. "That's all it says."

"Ridiculous!" Evangeline snorted. "That would be even worse casting than putting *you* in the part."

"But why bwing up *Anna Kawenina* at all? What has that to do with committing murder—or suicide?"

"Suicide—that's it!" Singer looked to us for confirmation. "Didn't *Anna Karenina* step in front of a train engine at the end of the film? Hell! There are so many main line stations in London—which one would she choose?" His expression became dazed at the multiplicity of choices. "Paddington? Euston? King's Cross? Victoria? Waterloo? I'll have to put out an all-points alarm and have them all watched."

"There's something awfully wrong here—" That torn sheet still bothered me. "I don't believe a word of this."

"Actually, neither do I." Evangeline scrutinized her note again. "Juanita Morez was a semi-literate with Spanish as her first language. She had to learn to speak more or less properly when the Talkies came in, but it was as much as she could do to write her name on a contract. All these words are spelled perfectly—and English spelling, at that."

"And she never got nearer playing *Anna Karenina*—" I was following my own train of thought—"than the time she was tied to the railroad tracks in *Rails Going Westward*—"

Suddenly, the torn sheet began to make sense. People were always tearing up sheets to use as bandages—or bonds—in the early films.

"Are there railroad tracks near here?" I demanded of Singer. "Is there a place where the rails run over open land, easily accessible? Never mind the big stations—that's where we should start looking for her. If we're not too late . . . if the trains don't run too frequently . . ."

"The Magic Wailway!" Gwenda cried. "It wuns over land of that descwiption wight by Pwimwose Hill!"

"What!" Evangeline glared at her suspiciously.

"The North London Wailway," Gwenda clarified. "People call it the Magic Wailway because it gets you fwom one part of London to another as if by magic. Also there's a twain when you least expect it. Oh, huwwy!"

"The car!" Singer dived for the stairs, we tumbled after him. He tried to outdistance us, but Gwenda slowed him down at the front door so that we could catch up. He yanked open the door and we hurtled past a couple of dark shapes at the top of the steps, nearly knocking them over.

"Mother! Where are you going?"

"I don't know—but don't get in my way!" We pushed into Sergeant Singer's car and roared off. Looking back, I could see Martha and Hugh hurrying down the steps and into Hugh's car to follow us.

"Why don't you radio for help?" Evangeline demanded.

"There's no radio, this is my own car," Singer said. "I thought I was off duty tonight."

We careened through the night, taking corners on two wheels. It was too bad the car didn't have a siren, either, we could have used one. The old movie trick of being chased by indignant patrol cars for that kind of driving also didn't work. There's never a policeman around when you need one.

"Here—" Singer thrust a powerful flashlight at Gwenda. "Shine the torch along the tracks. See if you can pick up anything." He slowed the car as we ran parallel with some railway lines crossing level land.

"No, nothing. Twy the next—No, wait a minute—"

We saw it then. A large shapeless black blob lying across

the tracks. The car slewed to an abrupt stop and Singer
leaped out.

"It's twue! Oh, what a wotten thing to do to some poor
twain dwiver!"

"Speaking of which," Evangeline said practically. "When
is the next train due?"

"Oh, howwors! And we sit here talking!" Gwenda flung
open her door and dashed after Singer.

"Come along, Trixie—" Evangeline opened her own door
and stepped out. "We might be able to help."

"Not if we break a leg." We lurched over the uneven land
towards the pool of light by the tracks. I was dimly aware of
the squeal of brakes as another car pulled up behind
Singer's. Then we scrunched across the gravel bed and we
were at the rails.

"Gwenda—" Singer was working frantically. "Give one of
them the light to hold and untie her hands."

"Well!" Evangeline took the flashlight as I stepped across
the tracks to help Gwenda. "I never thought I'd play this
scene again. I'd have sworn it went out with D. W.
Griffith."

"It may be corny, Evangeline, but it can still be deadly," I
reminded her. "All it takes is for a train to come along."

Gwenda and Singer redoubled their efforts. I stared
anxiously both ways along the track.

"If you hear anything coming," Singer said, "start
swinging that light and try to flag them down." He clawed
desperately at the knots.

"Don't you have a knife?" Evangeline asked disapprovingly.

"Not even the police carry concealed weapons," Singer
said. "And just as well, or I might be tempted to get very
nasty when I get my hands on the one who did this. He
soaked the knots when he tied them to pull them tighter
and made sure she couldn't free herself."

The familiar scent drifted up from the sheeting, but there
was something wrong. Evangeline directed the light alter-
nately between the knots at the hands and feet while the
others worked, but no one was paying attention to what was
in between. Otherwise, they might have noticed that it

was about eighty pounds lighter and considerably narrower
than Juanita.

I crouched by the head and began to unwind the
sheeting swathed around it. Had the head been covered
because she was already dead? Or because she was alive
and someone did not want to face the accusing eyes if she
recovered consciousness? She was lying awfully still.

"What are you doing there, Trixie?" Evangeline swung
the light on me just as I loosed the last strip and pulled it
away. Blonde hair gleamed in the light.

"It's Anni!" Gwenda gasped.

"In that case," Evangeline said, "where's Juanita?"

I tugged at the gag and freed Anni's mouth. She wasn't
dead, but she didn't look well. I tried to remember Des's
technique with the Kiss of Life. We could have used him
now.

"Mother . . . Mother . . ." The banshee wail was carried on the wind as Martha and Hugh stumbled towards us.
For once, I was glad to see her. We needed every extra
hand.

"Over here!" I called "Hurry!" I checked the track both
ways again. There was still no train in sight, but we didn't
want to push our luck.

"Good Lord!" Hugh looked down at Anni and her would-
be rescuers. "What's going on here?"

The question was rhetorical. Even as he spoke, he pulled
out a Swiss Army knife, selected the largest blade, stooped
and began sawing at the stubborn cloth. Threads began
parting.

"Good man!" Evangeline approved of him for the first
time. "Now get her hands. Martha, rub her ankles and get
the circulation going."

"She's in a bad way, I'm afraid." Hugh's assessment
looked accurate. I'd be happier if she moaned—or moved at
all.

"Mother, what are you doing here? How did you know
about this?"

"We were looking for Juanita," I said. "She left a suicide
note—several of them—that seemed to indicate the railway. Only she didn't write them—and she isn't here."

"Juanita?" Hugh looked up sharply. "Then where is she?"

"She has probably run away," Evangeline said. "Leaving this—" she gestured to the prostrate Anni—"behind her."

"You think Juanita could have done this?" Hugh almost laughed. "Don't be absurd."

"The only absurdity," Evangeline said coldly, "is Juanita. Her head is so full of the old movies she made that this seemed the best way to dispose of a rival."

"Impossible," Hugh said flatly. The last strands parted and he began chafing Anni's wrists. "I'm not arguing," he said, as Evangeline began to speak, "that Juanita might not have *thought* of doing this. What I disbelieve is her physical capacity to implement the plan. She would have had to carry this girl across the wasteland to the track, then tie these knots so tightly we had to cut them. She couldn't possibly have done it. Could you?"

"Then she had an accomplice!" Evangeline avoided the distasteful question.

Unwillingly, I thought of Des. First Mick, and then Des, disposing of the bodies for an evil crazed old lady. The strong healthy boys, lending their strength to protect her from the consequences of her madness. And look at what had happened to Mick.

In the distance, a train whistle sent its melancholy two-toned whoop into the night.

"Get her off the track!" Singer ordered. He and Hugh lifted Anni clear of the rails and set her down parallel with the track. Martha covered her with her coat.

We stood there, feeling a sense of anti-climax, listening to the approaching train.

"Is that on the uptrack or the downtrack?" Hugh asked uneasily.

"Of course!" Evangeline was galvanized into action. "There are *two* sets of tracks!" She moved forward, swinging the flashlight to provide the widest arc of light.

"The train—" I stumbled in her wake before the men could move. Perhaps because I had known her for so long, I could follow the way her mind worked. Gwenda followed me.

"Down there!" At the farthest edge of the ray of light, we could just discern another dark shapeless mass on the other track. "We've found her!"

The men came running in response to Evangeline's call, leaving Martha to look after Anni. The train whistle sounded again—much closer.

This time there was no doubt that it was Juanita. Her black eyes flashed fury and relief above the gag covering her mouth.

These knots slipped easily. They had her free and clear of the track just as the train approached.

"In the nick of time . . ." Singer said shakily.

"Just like the old movies," Hugh agreed grimly.

Then some fool took the gag off Juanita's mouth and the night turned blue with her comments—in two languages.

CHAPTER 20

We left Anni and Juanita at the hospital; Anni in intensive care. It seemed that she had been unconscious over several days and there was a build-up of sleeping pills in her system. *My* sleeping pills. Juanita, although bruised and bearing multiple abrasions from having been dragged along the gravel bed, was in better shape but was being kept in for observation at, I suspected, Heyhoe's instigation. After taking her statement, he had plainly had enough of her to last him the rest of his life.

It was Gwenda who worried me. She was badly shaken and still incredulous. They were her flatmates and friends, she had never seriously suspected any of them.

Once more the police car drew up at the foot of the steps. We were immediately behind it in Hugh's car. Beside me, Gwenda shuddered.

"And now," Evangeline announced with relish, "for the final scene."

Gwenda broke abruptly. She took a deep breath, turned towards Evangeline and shot off a volley of English and Welsh words full of lilting l's and rolling r's. The language was obscure, but the meaning was clear.

"There now!" Evangeline said triumphantly. "I knew she could speak as well as anybody else if she put her mind to it!"

Gwenda l'd and r'd her some more and leaped out of the car.

"Was the lisp bothering you?" Hugh asked in surprise. "It's just an affectation a lot of the kids have these days. It's supposed to be an Edwardian accent. Gwenda does it because it keeps her from lapsing into a Welsh accent. Don't worry, it's nothing permanent. If she got an offer from the Royal Shakespeare Company, she'd forget it tomorrow."

"So I can see," Evangeline said drily.

The police were already at the top of the steps. Gwenda opened the door for them and followed them in. Hugh didn't wait for us, he rushed up the steps, leaving Martha, tight-lipped, to open her own door and then ours.

"I suppose he telephoned Beau from the hospital," Evangeline said, "like a proper little go-fer and toady."

"What are you talking about?" Martha snapped. "Hugh Carpenter is one of London's most successful producers. He has three shows running in the West End right now. Where did you get the idea he was working for Beauregard Sylvester? I can assure you, the shoe is on the other foot!"

"Well—" Evangeline had been corrected, but not daunted. "He certainly gives the impression of being a go-fer."

"He's been trying to help Sylvester clear up his financial problems to free him to work in a new play. *You* ought to know—" Martha was scathing—"how much *some* actors need people dancing constant attendance on them!"

At a less fraught moment I might have cheered them on, but I decided to save my breath for the stairs. It was a long haul up to the top flat.

"Des!" I greeted him with relief as we entered. "You're all right! I was getting worried about you."

"Just working late." He jingled his pockets and winked at me. "It was a good night."

"You must have been the only person who had one," Gwenda said. "*Our* night has been terrible!"

And it wasn't over yet. The police were searching the flat. Hugh went downstairs and brought back Jasper, in pyjamas and half awake.

"What's going on?" Jasper demanded. "What's happened now?"

"Nothing—" A policeman came out of the kitchen and shook his head at Heyhoe.

"All her things are still in there." Singer came out of the bedroom. "She's either flown the coop in just what she was wearing, or—" He shrugged.

"That's Ursula's room!" Des stepped forward. "What were you doing in there? Where is she?"

"Just what we'd like to know," Heyhoe said. "Anyone got any ideas?"

"Ursula?" Jasper seemed dazed. He looked to Gwenda, huddled in a corner of the sofa. "Has Ursula disappeared, too?"

"Ursula," Evangeline informed him crisply, "had good reason to disappear. She killed two people and has just tried to kill two more—one of whom was your grandmother."

"My grandmother?" Jasper turned to Heyhoe. "Is she serious? What's happened to my grandmother? Where is she?"

"In the hospital," Heyhoe said. "She'll be all right. No thanks to your friend, Ursula, who tied her to the railway tracks."

"But very lightly," Evangeline pointed out. "Unlike Anni, who was tied very tightly. Obviously, Ursula intended to return after the train had gone by and remove Juanita's bonds. Then it would look as though *she* had tied Anni to the tracks and been caught by a train coming the other way as she left Anni. As a fail-safe, there was the reference to *Anna Karenina* so that you could take your choice between suicide or a fatal accident. Very clever, our Ursula."

"Quite so," Heyhoe said. "Especially the way she used the old movie methods of killing off people—or seemed to. I must admit—" he bowed towards Evangeline—"my first suspicions were directed to you."

"By a very expert hand." Evangeline granted pardon. "Eventually, I'm sure you would have realized your mistake. A woman who spent her days restoring old films has her head filled with the early cinematic visions more surely than the elderly actresses who played the original roles. After all, we have moved on in time, done other things, and are looking to the future. We can hardly remember most of the roles we played. But they were all fresh in her mind."

"And *she* thought she'd have a twy for Beau. That's why she killed Fiona and twied to kill Anni."

"Why she killed Fiona perhaps—" Evangeline said—"and put her in Des's bed until she had a chance to dispose of the body. Only Mick came along and found Fiona there and saved her the trouble."

"*My* bed?" Des squeaked; he was miles behind us.

"Except that she then had to dispose of Mick before he began questioning the situation," Heyhoe supplied. "She had free access to deadly chemicals always available in a photographic lab. We've had the autopsy report; he was poisoned and, as a finishing touch, she scalped him, since Miss Sinclair was living on the premises and the film premiere was still fresh in everyone's mind."

"I can't believe she'd be so wotten! I mean, Ursula! I thought we knew her, we were fwiends—"

"She tried to kill me," I said. "Of course, she thought I was Juanita. I suppose she had no real faith that Beau *would* go through with that divorce and she thought she'd short-circuit the process."

"Dear Beau," Evangeline said. "Even though he moved away from a place with Community Property Laws, a divorce would still be an expensive proposition for him. That would bother him more than keeping the marriage going."

"Obviously, you knew him well." Heyhoe could not resist the crack. Singer looked up hopefully.

"Evewyone knew that," Gwenda said. "*And* he's been in financial twouble wecently. He'd never choose *this* time for a divorce—no matter what he told Fiona or Ursula."

"Fiona may have believed him, but Ursula would have known better." Jasper had a wry smile for his grandfather's naughtiness.

"She also had a pretty shrewd idea that the next woman who married him would be left a rich widow," Evangeline said. "Even with a goodly portion going to Jasper, Cinema City is an inheritance not to be sneezed at."

"She did love old films so," Gwenda said sadly.

"You have to give her that," Evangeline agreed. "But she got too immersed in them. There's no point beyond which affection becomes obsession. I doubt if she'd have been so interested in Beau if he hadn't represented so many past glories. Once she'd lived with him for a while, she'd have opted for an earlier widowhood than she'd planned. He's had a lucky escape—but I don't suppose it will persuade him to change his ways."

There were footsteps on the stairs and one of the policemen who had been searching the garden came in and went straight up to Heyhoe. He spoke softly, but I caught the words, "bin liner"

I drifted over to the window and saw lights at the bottom of the garden, by the bench where Mick had rested. They were gathered around a black plastic sack and men were busy with it, but unhurriedly. There was no rush about it.

Poor Ursula, poor obsessed child. Another Hollywood victim, later and in a different way from the usual run, but Hollywood had claimed her, none the less. I hoped she had seen some splendid visions as she pulled the darkness of the sack around her and drifted away.

"Mother—Mother—" Martha was plucking at my elbow. "Mother, Hugh has something to ask you—and I want you to consider it very carefully."

"Don't tell me he's about to ask your mother for your hand," Evangeline sneered.

"I hardly think that's necessary," Hugh said coldly. "And, if it were, I wouldn't know which of you to ask."

"Don't look so stricken, Mother," Martha said. "I think I've always known."

"I don't know what you're talking about," Evangeline said coldly. "You can't be egocentric enough to imagine *I* could have whelped you!"

My hands were around her throat before I realized I had moved. For the second time in our lives, we were deep in a knock-down drag-out fight—and I was going to murder her if I could. I was gripped by the same deadly fury that had gripped me on the far-off day when she had coolly informed me that she was going to have a baby by my husband but, since it would be embarrassing professionally for her to produce a change-of-life baby, she would graciously allow me to bring it up.

"Mother—let go! Mother—!" Which one of us was Martha appealing to?

"All right, that's enough!" Hugh's arm enveloped me, pulling me away. Singer had seized Evangeline and was leading her to the far side of the room.

Heyhoe beamed upon us both impartially. If he applauded, I'd try to kill him, too.

"That settles it," Hugh said. "I want you both for a revival of *Arsenic and Old Lace*—and I won't take no for an answer. You can do a limited run, if you like, and you won't have to do matinees—but I must have you."

"Oh!" I shook myself free and tidied my hair. "Well, I'll have to think it over."

"Please, Mother," Martha said. "I'd like to stay in London for a while. And I think it would be marvellous for you to do stage work again." It must be serious with Hugh.

"Well . . ." Evangeline said consideringly. "It might work out rather well. Detective-Sergeant Singer wants to write my biography. Collaboration would be so much easier if we were in the same country."

"Just one thing—" I said. "Isn't there a nice little ingenue part in that? If you'll let Gwenda—"

"Yes," Hugh smiled. "I think that can be arranged."

"Cwumbs!" Gwenda said. "That's tewwific. And the day after we open, *I'm* taking *Twixie* to lunch!"